THE DEMON WAY:
BLOOD MOON

MADELYNNE ELLIS

KELL'S PROPHECY

When the Blood Moon rises, the demons' prince will wake from his thousand-year slumber and cast a shadow across the sun. The city will become *youkai* paradise, a vast playground of perversity and vice. However, his rebirth will encompass many stages, during which time we will know him only by his mark."

1. BLOOD FEVER

THE SOUND OF pursuit grew closer.

Sweat beaded every inch of Asha Lemarche's body, making her shiver despite having run full tilt for half a mile. Her plan had worked; most of the Talon had peeled off the bridge the moment they'd spotted her. More importantly Blaze hadn't made too much fuss over her leaving. She hated lying to him, but he wouldn't have gone if he'd known she wasn't joining him on the other side of the bridge.

Deep down, the fact she'd allowed Blaze to cross over appalled her. What choice had she in the end? Better that he was as far from Talon as she could get him, even if that did mean placing him in the hands of her long time enemy.

How her world had changed in the space of a few days—trusting a demon to keep her lover safe... Asha shook her head, correction—

trusting a demon to keep another demon safe. She'd gone way beyond consorting with the enemy. She'd allied herself with their prince. More than that, she was in love with him.

She could no longer pretend otherwise. For years she'd hidden behind an icy veneer, but here in the dark, on her own, fearing for Blaze's safety rather brought things into perspective. A bond had formed between them. She hadn't sought it, but it had grown nonetheless, so now their fortunes were irrevocably bound to one another and the rise of the Blood Moon.

If only she knew for certain that Blaze and Raven had safely crossed the bridge.

Asha kicked hard, but there was no power left in her limbs. She'd already pushed her body to the limits of endurance. The effort sent her temperature rocketing so high her vision blurred and a ferocious buzzing started inside her head.

She staggered onwards, fighting the dizziness, until the spongy marshland gave way to the warehouse district, where rolling mounds of abandoned rubble overgrown with weeds bordered derelict buildings. Only the yellow brick units up by the crossroads and those on the edge of the Birdcage remained in use.

Asha slid into the shadows that lined the pitted walkways between the buildings, no longer capable of maintaining her earlier gait. Fire filled her chest making it impossible for her to recapture her breath. Her best hope was to hide and pray she could stay quiet enough for her pursuers to pass her by.

Another block on, she found a gap in one of the corrugated iron walls. "Nuisance skirts!" It took a bit of wriggling, but she managed to squeeze through. There were no lights within, and only a few scant rays of moonlight penetrated the opaque skylights. Still, there was something soothing about the dark.

If she could only lie down against the cold earth.

While she stood assessing her options, too afraid of falling to move a step, the sounds of numerous booted feet passed along the alleyway outside. Damn, she'd hoped they were further behind her than that.

Familiarity with the Talon's methods didn't help with her jitters. They'd spread out and search the area quadrant by quadrant, the same way they hunted the youkai.

No sense in running, they'd only hear her. A nice dark corner was definitely her best option.

Cold sweat trickled down her spine. The steel boning in her bodice pinched. Asha sucked in a breath, inflating her lungs against the restraint, but she remained light-headed and unable to move. Who was she kidding? She wasn't going anywhere.

The iron wall behind her sighed as it slid open on long rusted runners. A figure filled the narrow opening.

"Asha?"

Jaku. Her ex-partner's voice rang like an alarm in her head. It echoed and clanged, but then the shuffle of her own feet as she turned to face her former partner also made her ears ache.

He alone filled the gap. She'd expected him to arrive with backup, but maybe this was better.

"Where is he?"

Asha stripped off her gloves and drew her hand across her sweat-peppered brow. "With any luck on the other side of the bridge."

"You played decoy for that youkai whelp? Asha, I know he's pretty, but really."

Speaking of pretty, she couldn't remember the last time Jaku had appeared quite so radiant. He emerged out of the gloom so that he stood below one of the skylights. He'd always taken excessive care of his appearance, but tonight he'd truly surpassed himself. Black brocade ruffles edged with lace flowed over his slim hips. The sleeves of his tight fitting jacket buttoned with slivers of jet all the way to the elbows, while yard upon yard of elaborate beading decorated the front. The only flash of colour in his entire appearance was the bright red of his lipstick.

A fist sized pitch black stone sat at the base of his throat, mounted upon what looked suspiciously like a collar.

"You've betrayed us. Betrayed every value you ever had, and for what?"

She blinked slowly, recognising the whisper of steel against sheath as he inched his sword from its scabbard.

"I'm not the one that ran Talon through

with a halberd, o' paragon of virtue," she chastened him. Did you know he'd survive, or were you hedging your bets?"

Jaku drew another inch or two of steel.

"Why'd you do it, Jaku? Who exactly is he helping by pursing this war, apart from himself? Blaze doesn't want to fight, and he wasn't seeking a crown until we put the notion in his head."

"He had the prophecy."

"He had an ancient manuscript that he couldn't even read. All he wanted was resolution and some connection to his past. One of the first things he told us was that he'd recently lost his grandmother. Everything else that happened was down to us."

Jaku lunged forward, but he stopped short of striking her. "I should kill you."

"You don't want me on your conscience, Jaku. There's not room in your heart for any more guilt."

Jaku drew himself up sharp. He had a good foot of height on her, forcing her to peer up at him in a way that strained her neck if she wanted to maintain any sort of eye contact.

"What's Vervain told you?"

"Nothing. He didn't have to. Do you really think I've stood back to back with you for years without working it out? It's in the parish records. All your family died on the same day, you can't pretend that's not a little suspicious. And on top of that, you've never once mentioned them by name. Not ever."

His nostrils quietly flared.

"You could have talked to me about it any time. I thought maybe one day you would."

All trace of friendship fled his face. "Raise your weapon."

Asha laughed.

A low growl escaped Jaku's throat.

She placed her hand on her sword hilt, but there was no drawing it. She hadn't even the strength to properly form her grip.

"Draw your sword."

"It's not happening." Limbs impossibly heavy and her head equally light, she swayed. Blaze was in danger. She could sense it. Taste his fear and confusion. Blood and fire swam across her field of vision. Then all the lights went out.

"ASHA!" Jaku caught her as she crumpled. He lowered her gently to the floor still cradled in his arms. The pulse in her neck was weak and flighty, and even without removing his gloves he could sense the clamminess of her skin. "Asha?"

What had that youkai bastard done to her?

She groaned as he lifted her eyelids. The pupils were contracted to pinpoints, making her eyes almost entirely green. So green she looked poisonous. He sniffed, and searched for wounds but there were no visible incisions and no signs of poison, beyond the reek of demon stink, that is. Blaze's scent was all over her;

musky and spiced, and strong. Too goddamned strong.

He should have dealt with the boy when he'd had the chance.

Jaku opened Asha's mouth. Although her tongue was swollen there was no obvious sign of foul play.

He absolutely was going to kill Blaze Makaresh when he found him.

Jaku stroked a hand through Asha's hair. Many of the long strands had come uncoiled from their pins and hung in matted tangles. She was a mess, almost unrecognisable compared with the perfect porcelain doll image she usually presented. "What the hell happened, Asha? What did he do to you?"

He'd spent years admiring her and trying to duplicate her elegance. He'd wanted to be her. He'd craved every nightmare caress Talon had bestowed upon her. Even now, when he'd taken her role, he still envied her. He wasn't fool enough to think Talon actually valued him. His recently elevated position was merely a means of controlling him lest he turn traitor, as Asha had done.

"Maybe I should end it for you now. You might even thank me for it," he said, stroking her pale face.

As if he could ever summon the strength to do it.

Jaku sensed Talon's arrival long before the metal doors screeched open again, and the scents of holly and myrrh penetrated the still air.

"What have we here?"

"She's ill." Jaku distrustfully hunched himself around Asha's prone form.

"So protective." Although his master's voice was barely more than a whisper, it nevertheless carried in the still air and bounced back to them as a hissing echo. "It's sweet. But I'll take her now."

Talon touched his shoulder, then lifted Jaku's chin, forcing him to meet his gaze. "Give her to me."

"Why do you want her?" He kept her cradled tight against his chest. "What are you going to do to her?"

The ghostly smile troubling Talon's lips curved into something infinitely more readable. "I'm going to take her home, Jaku. You said yourself she's ill. This deserted hangar is no place to treat her. Come, help me. Hold tight to me and we'll all go together."

Clinging to Talon's wrist, Jaku felt the wind rush around them. The earth shifted beneath his feet and within the blink of an eye they'd exchanged one cold cavernous room for another. Around them, flames lit, throwing gilt sparkles over the sumptuous ruby-coloured décor.

Talon glanced at the bedclothes and they folded back upon themselves. "Lay her on the bed."

Jaku set her down softly. She blinked as he rested her head upon a pillow and muttered another groan. Her eyes opened unnaturally wide, but he wasn't sure if she could see him.

Her irises still remained that unnatural shade of venomous green; the pupils mere pinpricks. Humans weren't supposed to have eyes like that. He wasn't sure anything had eyes like that.

"It'll be all right, Asha. We'll take care of you." He clasped her fingers between his hands and squeezed. "She's burning up." He said to Talon, turning to seek him out. "We need to cool her down."

Over by one of the two heavily laden tables, Talon stood pouring a red, viscous liquid into a goblet. "I'm not interested in treating symptoms, Jaku. What's important is establishing the cause of her malaise."

"Youkai poison." He knew that already.

Talon crossed to the bedside. He sniffed as though he were wafting the smell of wine into his nostrils and not demon stench. The reek remained distinctive and unmissable. "She's certainly been busy with the demon whelp. You don't smell like this without some serious body contact."

Asha, you fool! Jaku silently chastised her. He'd berate her properly once she was well again. After years of seeing what these beasts could do, of having to deal with the screwed up addicts who only lived for another fix of Blood Rain, and who would willingly screw a demon every night, allow them to bite and feed, take whatever they wanted, she really ought to have known better. She did know better, he knew she did, and yet Blaze had still got to her.

For her own safety, he ought to have separated her from Blaze the moment he'd realised what Blaze was. Correction—he ought to have separated Blaze's head from his shoulders.

Asha had always had a taste for Blood Rain.

Talon had even encouraged it.

Made use of it.

Controlled her with it, offering it to her on a teaspoon before they had sex. He knew. He'd watched and listened to her squeals of agony and ecstasy as she and Talon fucked.

This was as much Talon's fault as it was his, or Asha's.

'You should never have got her hooked on that stuff. Why would you do that? Why poison her with the very thing we were working so hard to stamp out?"

Talon stared down at his nose at him. "I don't need to explain my reasons. Leave us."

Why?" Jaku straightened to his full height. In years of servitude, he'd never once challenged Talon's authority, but today it had become habitual.

'Because some things are best accomplished in private, that's why. Trust me, Jaku, Asha would agree. She wouldn't want you to bear witness."

"If you hurt her—"

"Why would I hurt her? She's far too precious to me."

"Then what are you going to do?"

Talon lifted the crystal goblet he was holding. "Give her some medicine." His smile bordered on grisly.

Jaku hesitated, still stroking his hand across

her clammy brow. He didn't trust Talon. Not one bit. But he also understood the sense in choosing one's arguments carefully.

"I'm not going to kill her, Jaku. If that were my intention, I wouldn't have brought her here to do it. I'd have left her in that drafty warehouse. The thing with bodies is that you have to dispose of them. I may enjoy a fetish or two, but I've no desire to have a dead girl in my bed."

The reassurance, if that's what it was, didn't exactly quash Jaku's worries, but he knew from Talon's expression that reasoning with him would achieve nothing, and meanwhile, while he resisted, Asha further suffered.

"All right," he agreed. "I'll leave." No point stomping his feet over something this minor. It'd be like asking to have his head amputated for toothache. But he'd wait right outside the door and listen. The first hint he got that something untoward was occurring and he'd be back in this room and on top of Talon.

"I have to go now, Asha. Rest easy." He gave her hand a squeeze, before leaning over to brush his lips against her forehead. Even her breath tasted of youkai. "Talon has promised to take care of you." He intended to make sure that promise was kept.

TALON WAITED UNTIL he heard the door close behind Jaku before further examining Asha. Undoubtedly the masochistic fool would stay outside the door with his ear pressed to the wood in the same way that he'd always done. But then Jaku had always been a masochistic fool.

Asha lay still as death. Only the very faint rise and fall of her chest and the sheen of sweat on her brow convinced Talon she still clung onto life. Gently, he brushed the matted strands of hair away from her face.

"What have you done to yourself?"

He leaned closer and grazed his lips against hers. The cause of the fever was obvious enough. He'd seen her like this before on the downslide after a particularly impressive Blood Rain binge. Not that Blood Rain poisoning was responsible on this occasion. This was plain old Blaze poisoning, no doubt obtained direct from the source. The herbalists typically cut Blood Rain with all sorts of other shit, but even when it was pure he doubted it gave quite such an impressive high as she was currently experiencing.

He clucked disparagingly. "Really, Asha, you ought to know better. Didn't I teach you anything? You're not supposed to fuck them."

Well, there was only one thing for it. He wasn't sitting through days of her shivering, raging and acting like she had ice cubes in her pants. Talon slid a long slender knife from a holster strapped to his thigh, and then sliced it across his palm.

The flare of pain sent a shiver right down his spine and gave him an interesting if not entirely pleasant buzz. Warm blood oozed from the cut and rolled between his fingers. He held his palm over the goblet he'd already laced with alcohol and listened to the sizzle as his tainted blood hit the contents.

No more scraping demon remains off the floor to feed to her. He had something infinitely superior on tap.

Talon licked the knife wound and watched his palm slowly heal. Then he manoeuvred her into an upright position against the mound of snowy pillows and pressed the goblet to her lips.

She blinked slowly. "Time for your medicine. Drink now, Asha. You know it'll make you feel better."

The moment the mix of blood and brandy hit her tongue, her eyes opened.

"No!" She feebly lifted a hand to bat at his arm, but there was no strength behind the protest.

Talon kept the goblet angled, so the liquid dribbled into her mouth and over her chin. "Come now, if you will insist on fornicating with a demon, you have to be prepared for the consequences."

"No." She shook her head, but he grasped a handful of her hair and forced the issue.

"No, I really do insist, Asha."

She choked and spluttered, staining his bed sheets, but more than enough went down her throat. Already she felt less clammy, and a little colour had returned to her cheeks.

"No more." She damned him in a language she couldn't possibly know, so that each thread of sound wrought a scar across the ether, and made the universe howl.

Talon clutched his ears and glared at her. "Stop that, you ungrateful witch. Unless you truly want a war of words in the old tongue?"

She stopped. Gaped at him. Looked on the verge of an ear piercing scream.

"You've gone too far this time, Asha. This is the only way to bring you back."

She kept on shaking her head, leaving him unsure if she was questioning the honesty of that statement, or stating that she didn't want to be clean. In all honesty, he wasn't sure he could cure her addiction to Blaze. Demons had a way of getting under the skin, and Blaze was no ordinary demon.

Talon pinched her nose and forced more of the medicine down her throat. When she then retched, he pinned her down, spreading himself over her prone form.

"Don't you dare. Keep it down, Asha. It's important. We've been here before, remember? It's best you just do as I say."

All the previous times—when he'd had her sup Blood Rain from his navel and then sat unmoved while she'd begged him for a single touch, and when they'd fucked past the point of exhaustion until all the pain in the world went away—had been mere practice runs for this moment. Without him, she'd be dead now. OD'd on the youkai poison currently running through her veins.

She cried out, and he knew what she needed. "You do hunger, don't you?"

That was the problem with addicts; they always craved a little more.

He drew back the bedclothes and stroked a hand over her breasts and the hook and eye fastenings of her bodice. "And now that your little prince has used and abandoned you, I'm the only one who can give you what you need."

"Not abandoned... He's with me... I can feel him."

"Really? I think that's the poison talking, Asha. I imagine you crave his touch right now, but he's left you, and he's not going to come back and rescue you. He's the enemy, Asha. Our enemy. We've hunted his kind for a thousand years. We've kept the people safe. The Blood Moon is coming. You have to be strong."

"He will come. He's not like the others."

"You're right. He's far more dangerous than any of them. He has to die, Asha. We can't allow him to rise to power. Do you want the city to burn, to exist only as glowing embers beneath an eternally dark sky? They'll kill us and they'll feast. Slake their hunger with human flesh. They'll fuck us and feed on us, and we'll be mere slaves to their will. And you know how that feels, don't you, Asha? Because you already know how deliciously it burns to feel their bite and to have their blood upon your lips."

He leaned closer, so that his lips grazed the lobe of her ear. "My blood on your lips. You didn't think I was going to let you go without a fight now, did you? You're mine. Our relationship ends when I say it does and on my terms. You can forget your demon whelp, the only cock you need is mine."

2. MEMORY ZERO

"He who becomes the Burning Prince,
is born of fire into the human world.
He is a thing apart, not youkai,
but not entirely human either."
--Kell's Prophecy, The Apostle's Dialogue.

HE'D OVERSLEPT. Blaze knew it from the languid haze that hung over his head and the parched tickle in his throat. They'd been running. He recalled falling and staring up into a curiously familiar face with tawny oval-shaped eyes and a sweep of black hair shot with silver.

Sorrow.

The name reverberated inside his skull and made him smile because he knew something with a certainty he hadn't experienced since he'd first set eyes upon Asha and his world had fallen apart. Maybe things were working as Raven had predicted, and more memories would resurface the longer he spent here.

He blinked open his eyes. Wouldn't hurt to jump-start his memory with a little visual input.

He lay in a purple bubble of light cast by dozens of weeping beeswax candles, the scent of which permeated the air with a cloying, slightly sickly odour. The ceiling overhead was vaulted, church-like, save for the proliferation of leering imps carved into damn near every inch of stonework. Fascinated, he idled away a few minutes following the twists and turns of the elaborate carving, trying not to get creeped out by the fact that the imps moved. Not while you were looking at them mind; it was corner of the eye stuff only.

He shook off the jitters and gave a small snort. Hell knows where he was. There wasn't a smidgen of familiarity about the place beyond a passing resemblance to some of the fiery figures he'd seen on the Division Bridge.

If this was home he wasn't feeling a deep connection, but it certainly beat the last few places he'd rested his head.

Giving his muscles a bit of a workout, Blaze stretched and pushed upright into a sitting position. Someone had stripped him naked and given him a bed bath, judging by the distinct lack of odour coming from his armpits. Unfortunately, they'd also given him a once over with some bronze-glow moisturising shit, unless weirdly shimmery skin was the next stage in his metamorphosis into the Flaming Prince, or whatever the heck it was they were calling him. Disgusted, he spat on his thumb and rubbed at the bronzed skin of his arm. It came off. Thank fuck for small mercies.

Next task, then, was finding a shower, so he

could wash the rest of the shit off. What was the deal with it anyway? Was making him shine like some piece of statuary supposed to inspire adoration in his minions or something? He seriously hoped sparkles weren't his normal state of dress, because they sucked.

What's more, they especially sucked over the top of all the charcoal scribbles that despoiled his torso.

"You're awake. 'Bout time, snoozy boy."

Blaze's gaze tracked towards a shadowy corner a few feet from the end of the bed. Now that he studied it, it appeared to conceal an arched doorway. A moment passed before the figure properly appeared, and his eyes adjusted to the gloom beyond the candles' range.

"Who's there?"

The gloomy silhouette stepped forward a pace into the light, revealing... He squinted at the bespectacled, wing-less figure. Was that Tawny Eyes from the bridge? Life was going to be tough if he had to remember two images for everyone he met. "Sorrow?"

"That a real memory or a short term thing 'cause you heard Raven say it?"

Wish I knew the answer.

"Are you Sorrow?" He really wasn't sure. The guy on the bridge had been tooled and decked out in scuffed chestnut leather. This guy was wearing the youkai equivalent of slacks and a pullover. The fact that the slacks appeared to be made from some sort of animal hide, and the pullover sported a—actually he had no idea what that thing was supposed to be—only exacerbated his confusion.

"I am. Not that I haven't masqueraded as my sibling once or twice. I believe Skaa is out skulking somewhere."

The emphasis he placed on skulking suggested that was his sibling's normal state of being.

Okay, so he was filing facts here. Sorrow, check... Has brother, another check. Tawny eyes, mostly black hair, cheekbones you could slide down and seriously pantomime villain eyebrows. If he could get a handle on one person at a time and remember the bits of them that stayed constant then he'd manage this.

"How many people have been told I'm back and that I'm—" He paused, to chew over the words. "—that my memory is fucked?"

"We've kept it quiet."

"Good." Although, that meant that either Sorrow or Raven was responsible for his bed bath and bronze glow, which was a little disturbing.

"Folks know you're back. They can sense your presence. No one's beating down the door yet, but give them time. You've been away from us so long that many of them have concerns, especially given how close we are to the Blood Moon. I'd anticipate a rebellion, if I were you."

Grand. Just grand. Last thing he wanted right now was to face an audience, let alone quell any sort of uprising.

"The aristocrats, that is," Sorrow clarified, having presumably guessed from Blaze's expression that he wasn't following the subtleties of what was being said. "The rabble wouldn't dare to be so presumptuous in case you looked at them funny."

Looking at them funny, Blaze concluded, likely incorporated blowtorch vision or some other form of extreme chastisement no longer at his disposal. Yep, facing a crowd was definitely way down on his list of fun entertainments, which neatly brought him to his top priorities: clothes, followed swiftly by posting a sentry on the bridge to watch for Asha.

Chances were he was fooling himself over that one. She wouldn't attempt the crossing, but it'd lessen his anxiety to know they were watching for her, and short of searching for her, it was the best he could do right now.

Besides, Asha was no doubt safer without him, and it wasn't as if she didn't know how to take care of herself. Damn clearest mental picture he had of her was of her poised ready to decapitate another youkai head.

Blaze flipped back the covers and got out of bed. "I need clothes. Scratch that. Point me in the direction of the shower."

Sorrow nodded towards an arched doorway in the back wall, this one not as dingy as the one through which he'd appeared. "Need someone to hold the soap?"

Blaze did a double-take at the guy over his shoulder. For the life of him he couldn't figure if he was being propositioned or merely being offered the assistance of a chambermaid.

Sorrow's expression didn't give a damn thing away either. The demon had unreadable down to the level of Kell's Prophecy. There was no sussing him without a key or years of in-depth study. The fact that he supposedly had that but it was filed behind a wall of fog really didn't help.

"Think I can work up a lather all by myself."

Blaze's bed lay empty. After a momentary pause while this detail sank in, Raven lurched forward, his chest throbbing with damn near heart-stopping anxiety. He'd had a hell of a time getting down the hall. Someone needed to organise a serious larvae cull. Buggers had burrowed into the stonework and were apparently breeding in there. If Blaze had gone walkabout—shit! It really didn't bare thinking about. The castle was looking more dangerous than the streets.

"He's showering."

Raven stopped short a foot from the bed, his head snapping to the side to take in the figure sitting cross-legged upon the floor— Sorrow. *Bastard.* "Is he okay?"

"Fine and dandy. Leastways, he's breathing and upright."

He took a few extra paces in the direction of the wet room, only to pause before he got to the door. Bursting in and standing over the guy while he soaped up was unlikely to provoke a warm reception, and it wasn't as if he wasn't protected in there. Anxious showering had never suited Blaze. He liked to take pleasure in soaping himself. The walls in there had both ears and eyes. "As long as he's not gone AWOL around the palace." Larvae aside, there were plenty of other dissidents and the last thing they need was a pissing contest over who should rule.

"Not sure he was too impressed with the shimmer glow," Sorrow remarked. He had an assortment of slender instruments spread around him on the carpet which he was using to adjust the cogs inside his pocket watch.

"It was what was at hand. I had to do something to keep him stable while he slept off the exhaustion." And the bronze goop had been there, whereas the massage oil hadn't. Convulsing due to a dangerous fever by the time they'd transported him from the bridge to the heart of the palace; Raven had dispensed with ceremony and brought Blaze's hunger under control with what was available. Namely, his hand. If Blaze had been conscious, sure, the options would have been broader, and Blaze would have had more say, but letting him burn up and fade away wasn't on the agenda.

Even after he'd soothed most of the feverish aches, Blaze had muttered in his sleep, repeatedly calling out for Asha.

"Where've you been, Raven?" Sorrow looked up from his tinkering, his head tilted expectantly. "General consensus was you'd been powdered."

Revulsion at the idea of being reduced to

dust and then snorted up someone's nose set his saliva glands watering like crazy as they tried to flush the taste of bile from his mouth. He slumped down on the warm spot on the bed Blaze had recently vacated.

None of them had known about his punishment. Blaze hadn't set a guard nor had his sentence recorded, which only confirmed his suspicions about why Blaze had locked him up in the first place. He'd have objected to the hare-brained scheme his prince had concocted, so Blaze had put him out of action before its execution.

"Raven?"

"It's not important where I was." He refused to meet Sorrow's gaze, even though ignoring it meant tolerating a glare that could probably bore holes in concrete. "Blaze is the important one, not me."

"Sure."

The attention eased a little, as did the pressure in his head. *Why didn't you want me around, Blaze? If you'd at least explained, given me a chance to react and object, we might not be walking so blind now.*

"I know his memory is shot, but you have a strategy, right? That's all anyone is going to be concerned about. They've been waiting a long time for this."

Strategy. It had been hard enough getting Blaze here in one piece. The guy barely knew who he was, let alone how to bring about their ascension. That, and unless something major had snapped into place since he'd woke, being in the palace hadn't sparked a whole lot of recall.

"It's not like you to be so quiet. Okay, let me rephrase. How much does he understand about the Blood Moon's rise? It doesn't matter about the rest. He'll pick up the important stuff in a few hours once the next frenzy hits him."

True enough. Once Blaze had fed and shagged everyone he happened upon for a few hours it wouldn't matter what he remembered from the past, the blood exchanges would fill in all the important basics. No one would blink over him forgetting a few details. Once a demon got as old as Blaze, they tended to get a bit fuzzy over the details.

However, it still rattled him that his best friend saw him as a virtual stranger.

"He's a blank slate, Sorrow. There's no plan. All he knows is what I've told him, and the few bits he's picked up from the Talon based on the vagaries of Kell's bollocks."

"It's not bollocks." Sorrow let his pocket watch drop from his closed palm, so that it bounced on the extent of its chain, and then began to swing, slowly, pendulum-like over his groin. The watch rode a slow lazy arc, its dual tick heart-like in its rhythm.

It wasn't until his nose threatened to collide with his lap that Raven shook off its mesmeric effect. After giving Sorrow a scowl that would put most humans into a coma, but which Sorrow shrugged off, he repositioned himself on the bed.

"You never did read the Apostle's Dialogue,

did you?" Sorrow opened the watch case and made another adjustment.

An apology would have been nice, you wanker. Bastard had pulled that mesmerism trick on purpose.

"Why would I waste my time on the visions of a caned human priest?"

Alteration made, Sorrow grinned and dangled the watch on its chain again. "That'd be why you think this rebirth is pure coincidence."

"Inconvenience, actually. The old Blaze would have had no trouble bending the City to his will. And that rogue Talon wouldn't have stood a chance." *Damn castle wouldn't be overrun with vermin either.*

"And yet, he never did. Wonder why that was, huh?"

Raven dug his fingers into the eiderdown. The problem with Sorrow was that he liked talking elliptically and he got a kick out of all the weird shit. *The Apostle's Dialogue, Wicked Time, Entropy for Fun and Profit...* He lived and breathed that stuff.

"You might not believe, but Blaze did. He understood that like Earth's seasons, the cosmos has rhythms, too. Only the Burning Prince can initiate the change necessary to tip the balance in our favour. Only he can bring about our ascendancy. And the Blaze you knew never laid claim to that title."

True enough. Strange that he'd never really considered the implications of that fact before. "All right, so now I'm paying attention."

Sorrow shot him a hard look over the top of

his glasses before pushing them up his nose. For a good few minutes he didn't speak, so eventually Raven gave up waiting for the punch line and collapsed back against the pillows.

"His death was a necessity."

"What?" He sat so quickly his abs screamed in protest over the jolt. Death was a whole different picture to rebirth, and rather more final. The Blaze he knew had never been suicidal, nor had he been a big risk-taker. He was a planner, executing things with absolute precision.

"It's why he got you out of the way."

So he could kill himself? Bollocks!

"Hang on. This is your expert assessment? If he's dead, how come he's generating enough steam to power an engine?" White arms of fog were curling around the archway that led to the wet room.

"You've not been with him all this time. So, I have to assume he removed you from the picture early on. You've been missing years, Raven, not a few months." Sorrow held him trapped within his gaze. "You've both been missing years."

Raven shrugged. "So? Most of you were probably glad to see the back of me, and it ain't like Blaze hasn't absented himself for short periods before."

"Fifty year absenteeism is pushing the boat out even for Blaze."

"Fifty—no way!"

"Fifty-three years, twenty-seven weeks, and three days. And no one looked because there wasn't any point. This isn't a typical rebirth. It's not about readjusting his body chemistry to cope with a long life span. He's been reformed anew."

Raven shook his head, hoping the action would somehow make sense of the notion. It didn't work. If it wasn't rebirth, what were they talking, some form of reincarnation? "Explain. Give me something I can work with."

"The Prince, our Prince, not the reigning Regent, has to be born to the human world. Emphasis on born."

He was hearing, but he wasn't digesting this. Not properly, anyway. It didn't tally up straight his head. Not that anything had been particularly straight since Blaze had freed him from the bindweed in the Hall of Ancients.

"The Blaze you loved is gone, Raven. They might look the same, but they're not. Kell's Prophecy speaks of transformation. Transformation, not rebirth. The Prince is born of fire into the human world. He's a thing apart, not one of them but not entirely one of us either."

So, reincarnation was right on the mark. Still, "You're telling me this human grandmother he's so fond of is real, not just a construct?"

Sorrow raised his hands before his face and steepled his fingers. "I can't answer that. I haven't heard him mention her, and I don't know how the process works. Maybe he did have a human childhood. What I can tell you is that his transformation isn't complete. He's still more human than youkai."

"What needs—"

"—to happen? Simple, he still needs another soul. Without it, he's no use to any of us. Well, other than as larvae bait."

3. GRACE

BLAZE KNEW HER the moment he set eyes on her through the wall of steam in the wet room. At least he knew her name and recognised her physical form. Beyond that there was nothing but a void.

"Grace?"

She pushed herself away from the fogged up terracotta tiles as he stepped out from under the multiple dragon's maw showerheads. Dark, hypnotic eyes fixed upon his face, her head tilted up so the sharp point of her chin was angled towards him.

She'd dressed in next to nothing, just a few scraps of white lace that covered one leg and her modesty. Her wings were two vestigial white plumes set high on her back and clearly incapable of supporting her weight, the

30

feathers as fluffy as cygnets, but the snowy-white of an adult swan.

"Raven said you were home." Her smile stretched across her face, crinkling the corners of her eyes and bringing a glitter to their centres.

Home. This wasn't it. Home meant security and comfort. Home was the place he'd shared with his grandmother. The memory of her flooded his senses. Her scent—apple-pie and ginger. His ten...twelve-year-old self sat on a deckchair in the sliver of sunshine that graced their little paved terrace at the back of the house. He sipped his lemonade while Grandma squeezed a steady stream of water from their laundry with the mangle.

The scene completely obliterated the shadowy recollection he had of Grace, and of being with her. Not that he had any specific reference points to their relationship, just a vague sense of knowing, and a few layered snapshots of tossed clothing, beds in disarray, her hands on his flesh.

He knew her touch, the taste of her lips. The way she smelled after a night of excess, semen staining her skin, alcohol fumes on her breath, and the marks of his possession all over her flesh.

They'd shared blood... and other things, more than once...but she was still a shadow beside his grandmother.

She held a towel out to him. Blaze took it and swirled it out behind him to wrap around his waist. Only, the moment his arms were outstretched, Grace pressed up against his chest, and started running her forked tongue over the inky swirls of his tattoo.

Talk about instant heat. Blood rushed to his groin, for a moment he was hers entirely. Then he remembered to breathe and his brain started functioning again. "Ah... Um, Grace..." Too much, and he really didn't know whether she was pushing things beyond the level of intimacy they usually shared or whether this was an entirely typical welcome.

He let go of the towel and tentatively pressed the tips of his fingers against her shoulder. "Grace."

"Yeah?" The licking continued as she headed downwards, her wicked, pointy tongue finding his navel and poking inside to tickle all the impossibly sensitive nerve endings. Blaze rose onto his toes as the stimulation sent a streamer of pleasure hurtling down to his groin, where it reawakened all the rowdy, sexual nagging he'd been experiencing back in the catacombs.

When her hand skirted over his hip and settled on his inner thigh, he was hard pressed to know what to do. His cock was yelling one thing, but the flashback to the catacombs had also reminded him this wasn't Asha.

His lover was still out there fighting to protect him and she deserved his loyalty.

Curiously enough, while thinking of Asha did nothing to calm his erection, it did neatly cauterize his fleeting attraction to Grace. He didn't want her touching him. He didn't want any exchange of life essence, or any sort of bond being re-forged between them.

"I've things to do."

They had foot soldiers flying about the City; surely some of them could be trusted and tasked to keep an eye open for Asha.

A sharp fingernail grazed the edge of his loins. Blaze closed his eyes, took a breath, and then pushed her away. When she didn't respond to a bit of light pressure, he resorted to a firmer shove, the force of which left her squirming about on the rainbow of wet slate underfoot, hissing and spitting at him like the snake she damn well resembled now he was in a position to view her without a filter of sexual longing in place.

Black diamond-shaped eyes stared unblinkingly at him. She scowled and her tongue flicked between her sharp fangs to tickle the dry surface of her lips. He held her gaze, refusing to flinch or back down. If he was the boss around here, he needed to damn well act like one or they'd be trampling all over him in no time.

"I'll come back when you're feeling more amiable."

"You'll come back when I ask you to, and not before."

She hissed at him again, before turning tail and scampering from the wet room on all fours, her bottom waggling and her petite wings stuck out from her back like an enormous bow. Blaze followed her spindly crawl into the bedchamber. As soon as she realised he was following, she made more of an effort to shift, getting to her feet to scurry through the outer doorway.

"You were warned," Raven called to her retreating back. The big demon lay sprawled across Blaze's bed; the only noticeable change in his appearance since their flight across the bridge the presence of a clean shirt and neatly tied hair. He rolled onto his side, propped himself up on one elbow. A teardrop pearl hung from one earlobe. "Feeling fresher?"

Blaze gave him a cautious nod that the demon returned with a grin.

Sorrow sat crossed legged on the tatty carpet by the bedside, where he appeared to be mending his watch. He glanced up as Blaze padded past him. "Clothes are in the closet."

Blaze rolled his stride in that direction, only to pause before opening the armoire doors. "Which clothes, the old ones or the old old ones? 'Cause I'd prefer the stuff I arrived in."

Sorrow put aside his mending. "You two are such pigs. The leathers are over there. "He twitched a bushy eyebrow in the direction of a wicker basket, from which the sleeve of Blaze's fringed jacket was poking.

"Great. Thanks."

"You're joking. That stuff needs incinerating."

A sweet metallic scent clung to the clothing he dragged from the basket. Raven watched him, a smirk plastered across his handsome mug. Damn, but it felt weirdly right seeing the guy draped across his bed, like it was habitual for them to hang out like this. Raven's gaze remained fixed on him too, completely disregarding his nakedness, like he'd seen it all before. They were comfortable enough to not worry about averting their gazes and hell, looking at one another sure beat staring at the ceiling, or focussing on the painstaking mechanical tinkering happening on the floor.

"We need to talk," Raven mouthed. He shot a wary glance at Sorrow.

Blaze wetted his lips. "Can you fetch me some grub?" he asked.

Sorrow glanced up at him over the rim of his specs. "Me?" He started slotting bits back inside the silver fob case. "If you want Grace back, just holler, she's probably camped right outside the door."

"I don't want Grace. I want—"

"Don't tell me, you like them voluptuous these days. No, that's not it. You like them well hung."

The demon's gaze flicked down to Blaze's groin and back up so fast, Blaze was sure the guy was actually embarrassed by the notion. Except, weren't the youkai all about sating their appetites with whatever was available? Then he recalled the reaction he'd caused on the bridge by tweaking Sorrow's feathers and instinct told him there was more to it than that.

"—food. I'm running on empty." Soon as his appetite was sated, he was ordering that recon team. "Bread, maybe a hunk of meat or cheese stuffed between a couple of slices, will be just fine. Pickles if you've got 'em."

The colour leeched from Sorrow's face. "Oh! Oh, right. I see. That sort of hungry. I thought you meant the other sort of grub." He took off his spectacles, rubbed the lenses clean on his shirt and replaced them, only to remove them again and stow them in pocket of his slacks. "I'll go talk to the kitchens about it. Have something brought up."

"You do that. Never know, a bit of brain food might actually set me right."

Raven curled up and started choking into the mattress. "You weren't right to begin with. I guess it must have been your lady that scoffed all the stuff I swiped from the delicatessens."

"Shut up." Blaze threw the lid of the wicker basket at him, which rather surprisingly hit. "That was hours ago."

"Barely."

"Guess rebirthing is hungry work."

Raven laughter ceased. "Yeah, about that..." He sat up slowly while Blaze shook the creases out of his jacket. "Hey, I know you're attached to the coat, but there are clean leathers and shirts in the cupboard. You might actually be more comfortable in them, that stuff is pretty rank." He lifted the leg of the trousers Blaze had dropped onto the bed.

Blaze looked at the black jumble he'd dumped onto the eiderdown and saw his point. The T-shirt was ripped and bloodied, and stank of sweat. The trousers were even worse, covered in a surface dusting of mud and gore, with all the shit that had come down on their heads in the catacombs ingrained into the seams. A huge scuff mark graced the rear, and had nearly torn through the hide. One shot at minor acrobatics and he'd be mooning his opponents. "All right, point taken."

He returned to the wardrobe. Maybe it was time to embrace his demon side.

4. THE DEMON WAY

**
"The youkai are not to be trusted.
Their cruelty and perversity know no bounds."
--Wise Words to the Young.
**

RAVEN GOT OFF the bed while Blaze had his back turned judging by the creak of the bed. Blaze continued to rummage through the wardrobe, trying to ignore the tingling of his nerves over Raven's approach.

"What's the plan, Blaze?"

"You're shitting me! You expect me to know? It's not come back." His memory remained as fuzzy as his head after the Martyr's day booze up. "I still don't have a fucking clue about who I am, let alone what you expect me to do about all this Blood Moon crap. Ruling the world isn't actually on my list of life ambitions."

"It should be."

"Well, it's not." He fastened the fly of the leathers he'd pulled on. They fit like a second skin, perfectly tailored to his shape. Guess there was no disputing they were his. "My only concern in this is keeping out of Talon's way. He's done quite enough damage to my hide already."

"You're going to sit back and watch him bring misery to the masses?"

"The masses are already miserable."

"Sorry, did I run down Hangover Street with somebody else? You're going to sit back and let him get away with that shit? There were women and kids among the corpses."

Truthfully, Blaze wasn't sure he'd ever forget the mangled bodies and the waterfall of red stuff running over the cobbles. But that didn't mean he wanted a head to head with Talon, even if the visions he kept having suggested a confrontation was inevitable.

"What do you care? They were human, not youkai."

His companion had the sense to shut his mouth for a second. Unfortunately, the silence didn't last.

"Blaze, it's our chance at ascendancy. There won't be another opportunity for a millennia, assuming there are any of us left by then. The humans have held power and have been set on our annihilation for centuries."

"And we've been feeding on them for longer. You can't blame them for defending themselves."

That and there was a small problem with the whole argument. He hadn't actually chosen a side yet. He was against Talon, but that was one man, not the entire race, and he really hadn't embraced the whole youkai-demon thing yet. If he sat down and thought too hard about certain aspects of it, they stuck in his gullet, leaving him with an uncomfortable case of indigestion.

"Blaze," the plea in Raven's voice finally prompted him to speak.

"What the hell is the incentive for me to make this my fight? I don't care if the Blood Moon rises. I couldn't give a fig who rules up here or below in the City, and everything I've heard about what demon rule will bring is damned ugly." Death, destruction... The thought of packs of youkai loose among the humans, feasting, fornicating with nothing to hold them in check. Hell, he wanted no part of it.

Unfortunately, the same images of his demon brothers smeared with human blood caused the annoying erotic burn that kept afflicting him to start up again. Sensibilities aside, he was developing a bit of a fetish for the red stuff.

Fuck! This nonsense was really starting to mess with his head. He was starting to think he'd have been better off staying alone and clueless.

No way was he leading the youkai anywhere near the City. They could stay right here and wait it out. The Blood Moon could rise and fall and everything would remain hunky-dory. They'd all wake up to the same sights and sounds as the day before.

If there wasn't an obvious threat, Talon wouldn't have anything to wage an attack against, and he and his dolls would fall back on their traditional modes of entertainment, like swanning about in costumes looking pretty and acting hard.

Really, there was no incentive to get involved.

"That's a real nice picture you're painting."

Blaze paused with one arm through his T-shirt. He kept forgetting Raven could see into his head. The guy's right eye burned like a blowtorch.

"Transformation, that's what the Blood Moon is all about. It heralds in the new age. You're the one, Blaze."

"It's not happening."

"Don't lay money on that."

Having tugged his clean T-shirt straight, Blaze turned his back on Raven and readjusted himself behind his fly. Damned erection wasn't giving up. In fact, he was hard pressed not to give it a welcome tug. "I want to send a recon team out for Asha."

"Fuck!" Raven wrenched the leather cord holding his topknot in place free of his hair, then scrubbed his fingers through the collapsing strands. "What the hell for? Didn't we already have this discussion? She's killed too many of us. She's not welcome here."

"I say she is."

"Blaze, you're about to go down in history as the biggest fucking pansy the youkai have ever known. Why do you think they're going to accept one of the Talon into their midst? Considering the crap I've just faced walking through..." He shook his head. "Dammit, Blaze. The aristocracy are twitchy enough, and your other subjects need a good kicking. Drag your thoughts out of her lace panties for a moment and think this through."

"I wasn't,' he protested. 'Okay, maybe a teeny bit."

He noticed his arms were trembling as he pulled on the battered jacket. The shiver continued once he'd shoved his fists into his pockets. If he ignored it, it'd go away. Shame the same couldn't be said about Raven and the rest of the crap afflicting him.

"Man, you seriously need to get a handle on your appetites."

Two large hands landed on Blaze's shoulders. Having coaxed him into turning so they faced one another, Raven took a deep sniff of him. Blaze sniffed too, but whatever odour Raven detected, and which had caused his mouth to set in such an uneasy, scowl remained undetectable to him.

"Know what a frenzy is?"

"No."

A flicker of a smile tugged at the edges of the scowl, but the sign of amusement didn't stick. Instead, Raven patted his shoulder like he was offering condolences. "No matter." A distinct echo of "you soon will" loomed in the wake of the comment. Blaze risked a glance into Raven's eyes, but there were no tell-tale clues there. The fire that sometimes ringed his right eye with an amethyst halo was missing, and in its place rested stony determination.

"You're not going to persuade me," Blaze said, intending to pre-empt another sally of swaying tactics. "If we go out and fight, it'll only lead to more carnage, and I've seen enough for a lifetime. If you want it so much, you take the lead."

"I would, if it were that simple, but I'm not the one."

Blaze uncomfortably shrugged off Raven's hold. He turned away, his hand clasped to his breastbone, where beneath his T-shirt the mottled sigil marred his skin. He briefly entertained the notion of cutting it out, except while it might remove the mark, he didn't think it'd kill the infection. That's what it felt like. That he'd contracted a disease, only no amount of medicine would cure him.

His skin began to itch, and his stomach growled loudly. "When's that sandwich going to arrive?" He swung back to face Raven, who didn't even attempt to make conciliatory remarks, and didn't offer to go find out either.

"Blaze, there's something you ought to know." Raven's voice, just above a whisper, acted like a burr on his senses that flipped him onto red alert. Whatever bombshell was about to be dropped, he just prayed it wasn't anything to do with Asha.

"Go on."

But whatever it was Raven had intended to say, he changed his mind at the last moment, and shook his head. "No—it doesn't matter. It can wait for now. You need to eat...and stuff."

The distinct pause implied the "stuff" was actually rather high on the agenda.

"Tell me."

Raven gathered the strands of his dark hair together and secured them on the back of his head. "It's not important."

The hell it wasn't. His hackles were thoroughly raised, but he refused to beg for whatever titbit of information Raven was playing him for. Blaze shrugged, "Fine, we'll forget it."

"Good."

"Yeah, good." Which left them staring at one another like two imbecile goldfish, mouths open but a distinct lack of words coming out. Blaze shoved his hands deep into the pockets of his jacket, but he couldn't quite bring himself to break eye contact. Fact was, the guy's mismatched eyes fascinated him, and considering how touchy-feely he was right now that wasn't a good thing. Sticking his paws where they weren't invited was likely to get him punched. Maybe. He hadn't forgotten the way Raven had sucked his fingertips back in the Eyrie.

"One sandwich." Sorrow barged into the room and stepped right between them to place a laden plate on the end of the bed as if their "don't blink" death match was a non-occurrence.

Maybe it was.

"I'll leave you to enjoy it. Cook says it's ham, but it's probably goat." He offered them both a smirk and left again.

The tension virtually crackled between them after that. Heat plumed in Blaze's armpits. Seriously, he needed out of here. If he had any idea what to expect, he'd go right now. Then again, could whatever was out there be any worse than what he faced here?

A flush crept up his neck from beneath his collar, and all his senses seemed to switch to red alert. Red spots floated across his visual field.

Red...

Blaze imagined the taste of each blood drop as it rolled across his tongue. Its metallic tang; the satisfaction as it hit his stomach. The singing in his veins grew increasingly insistent, causing the prickles around his neck to grow more pronounced, and a similar irritation to break out in other areas of his body, leaving him tingling from head to toe.

Blaze ripped off his jacket...wings were coming...Oh, yes!

And for once he didn't want to stop them. Sensitive things were feathers; just the rush of air across each quill could provide enough erotic burn to power a brothel.

His skin split. The muscles in his back strained and stretched. He fanned out his wings and touched one of the inky feathers. Yes! Another stroke and near trance inducing ecstasy washed over him. He wanted this. Needed to know exactly how much pleasure his body could handle.

At the same time it was crazy. Asha loomed large in his thoughts, her fragile wintry beauty, the wan smile upon her lips as she'd turned to go.

Blaze twitched as though he'd been slapped, and pounced upon the double wedge of meat and bread instead of Raven. As he wolfed down the sandwich, taking rapid bite after bite, he barely tasted the meat to know whether Sorrow's assessment of its composition had been correct.

It wasn't bloody enough; he knew that for a fact. He had to content himself with licking smears of pickle from his fingertips. The snack simply hadn't filled the hollow pit in his stomach. "Need another."

Raven shrugged his shirt off over his head. "What you need you're not going to find in a sandwich." He crooked his head to one side exposing his neck from collarbone to jaw. Beneath his skin lay the firm throb of his pulse.

Blaze stared at him gobsmacked, hardly able to comprehend what was being offered. Still dazed he started forward, only to pause, his hands splayed over the firm slabs of muscle that comprised Raven's chest. "No. Not with you. It ain't..."

"It ain't what, Blaze? This isn't heading any place we haven't been before. I know things have changed but I can't obliterate the past to match up with however you think we should behave now."

Although drawn, the way Raven's lip curled so that a sliver of fang showed suggested the offer wasn't entirely altruistic.

"I'm more than ready to satisfy your

craving." The other demon leaned into Blaze's touch. "Believe me, the longer you hold out the worse it'll get. Your choice: me or the whole damn compound. And believe me, if you go wandering you're going to get fucked in every sense of the word."

Well, when he put it that way...

"What's so scary out there?"

"Youkai—your subjects. Other stuff. Stuff you don't need to think about right now."

Raven stroked a hand over the fan of black feathers, causing Blaze's loins to throb with pent up energy. Fear, apprehension, and desire simultaneously flooded his senses, heightening the frustration that already had him itching to shed the clothes he'd only just pulled on. He gritted his teeth against the notion, trying to hold his rampant desire in check. Trying to prove to himself how strong he was, and how this raging beast inside of him wasn't going to take charge.

"Tell me."

"Grubs, ghouls."

Another touch from Raven. Shit! He was seeing shooting stars. Feeling them, too. Suddenly his mouth was full of teeth and he could see Raven's pulse fluttering just beneath the skin in his throat.

"It's what we are, Blaze. It's not a choice. It's a necessity."

He knew what Asha would say, she'd tell him to keep on fighting, to hold the lure at bay until his strength ran out.

"Trust me, Blaze. I've kept you safe so far. This is in everyone's best interest"

"I don't trust myself." His fingers curled, their tips digging into Raven's skin leaving behind pink impressions.

"You won't hurt me. Leastways not in any way I won't appreciate. I can heal, remember. It's not the same as feeding on her."

Temptation roared in his ears.

"Bite. Feed."

Asha's ghostly pale face, shadows ringing her eyes haunted his thoughts. He'd have to be so careful around her. Not let his desires run away from him or he might wake to find he'd consumed her whole.

Maybe this was the best way. Raven would brush off the wounds.

Raven's breath caught when Blaze leaned forward. Damn youkai bastard was anticipating this with pleasure.

"Do it, Blaze. Do it or I'm going to take charge and then we'll be doing things at my pace not yours."

Blaze bit hard, taking a piece of flesh along with the blood. Thick and cloying, with a metallic sharpness, the taste filled his mouth. Ruby droplets ran over his chin. Raven groaned in his arms. His eyes had closed and the muscles in his face had relaxed after the initial incision.

Blaze drew long and deep, growing increasingly intoxicated. Desire pulsed through him. He felt alive, invincible. All he needed now was something to take the edge off his raging libido, and he wasn't doing that with Raven. Not because he hadn't done that before in both his lives, if what he was reading into his absent past were correct, but because he didn't want that sort of complication in his life right now. Subduing an ache was one thing, juggling lovers another.

A hand slid inside his fly. Blaze summoned every ounce of strength he possessed but still couldn't tear himself away from Raven's neck. As he waged the internal battle, it dawned on him it wasn't Raven's hand anyway, since both his fists were clenched around the lip of the eiderdown. Additionally, the hand was too small, the grip too light. Blaze turned his head a fraction, still trying to keep in contact with the source of his satisfaction.

Grace.

When had she crept back in?

Did he care?

Pleasantly cool, her hand circled his shaft, and her thumb swept in an arch, back and forth, over the most sensitive spot on his entire body.

Blaze bared his teeth, incapable of making anything approaching a rational sound.

"My liege. I don't mean to cause displeasure," she soothed in response to the growl.

On her knees, she leaned in to both his and Raven's bodies, and somehow found a way to entwine herself around their lower limbs. Her dainty cheek rubbed up against his inner thigh. Sickeningly that was all it took to override his sense of propriety and loyalty. So, he lacked willpower, who cared? This was the other half of what he craved. The thing he needed to take control of himself and his form. Her tongue flicked out, dabbed at the head of his cock. Blaze closed his eyes as her heat surrounded him. He was putty, and her hands...their hands, because Raven had stopped knotting the sheet and begun staging a simultaneous assault, played across his feathers until every quill stood as erect as his cock.

The caresses became increasingly rough, and were soon interspersed with scratches and nicks. They ought to have hurt. Instead, wave upon wave of ecstasy hit him, propelled him into a frenzy of gorging himself on blood and sex.

Blaze shoved Raven down onto the bed and climbed astride him, dragging Grace along too. The petite demon wound her sinewy body around them both, and proceeded to smother every inch of his skin in kisses. In turn, Blaze smeared the blood he'd taken from Raven across her lips.

Lost in a landscape of black flames and crimson tides Blaze floated, soared. The sigil on his chest began to smoulder and glow. Somehow Grace managed to wriggle her way between him and Raven. He didn't dwell on how she'd managed it, or that Raven was clearly as excited as he. Instead, he narrowed his focus, jammed a hand between her legs and fumbled with her lacy garment a second or two before tearing through the mesh. With barely a wiggle his cock butted between her thighs.

As Blaze drowned in her heat, he ignored the rhythm of Raven's upward thrusts beneath him. It wasn't important. He just needed the satisfaction of finding a physical release.

Grace gave a gasp as he sank deeper, and another when he bit the gentle rise of her breast. "Yes," she hissed in unmistakable triumph. "Yes, take what you want, anything you need."

He didn't want her, but at this moment he sure as hell needed her. Rabid, that's what he was, and desperate. Blaze dug his fingers into her rear, lifting her up so he could slide in and out more smoothly. He fucked her with long, smooth strokes, then in quickening bursts as his balls started to tighten.

Raven was right there with them too

"How—how do you manage it—the hunger?" Blaze gasped, between licks at the wound he'd made upon Grace's breast.

"I fuck, Blaze. I take whatever I can, wherever I can get it. I don't let myself get so stoked that I can't control the hunger."

Of course—Raven had been taking little sips of blood from him since the moment he'd woken, small mostly innocuous sips. Enough to raise eyebrows, but nothing more.

"That, and unlike you I'm not in the middle of a transformation."

Good point.

He couldn't respond because Grace had her nasty tongue in his mouth, and the wholly demon-part of him thought it divine. While she kissed him, eventually drawing the caress over his chin and down his body to his oversensitive nipples, her claws wandered over the contours of his abs. She followed each raised line of ink, and when she'd exhausted them her nimble fingers skirted the perimeter of the demon mark on his chest.

Blaze inhaled sharply, waiting for the zap of lightening that had struck every time Asha had touched him there, but it didn't happen. There was no bond, no intense feeling of heat and union. His breath oozed from between his lips. Her touch had caused nothing more than an irritating tickle.

"Anything," she moaned, her voice a breathless whisper, while her palm pressed flat against the sigil. "Whatever it takes, I'm here. Use me—"

He wasn't stupid. She was up to something. No other way of interpreting why she'd chosen to press her hand against his chest in exactly that position. Blaze smiled, showing more teeth than he realised he possessed, and clamped a hand over her mouth to save himself from having to put up with anymore false declarations. He hadn't the breath to order her silence. Whatever connection she was attempting to make wasn't happening. He cast a glance at Raven. Hard to say whether he knew of Grace's intentions, but either way, he presumably knew what and why she'd attempted it. Yes, they were definitely going to be having words when this was done.

Grace sucked on the fleshy part of his fingers, so he curled the middle digit, letting her take it full into her mouth. The tiny prick of her fangs barely registered, although he knew she was sipping his blood. Stealing it, he supposed. He could hardly complain, considering they were locked together and he'd stolen some of hers.

Raven tweaked his feathers again and the responding roar in Blaze's veins quickly drowned out all the internal questions he had clamouring for attention. Instead, he let muscle memory and instinct guide his final thrusts. *One...two...oh, yes, exactly like that. Exactly, absolutely like that. Perfect. Completely, perfect.*

Every nerve, every muscle, tendon and sinew locked tight and then released. His climax left him staring at the event horizon, where he floated awed by the vast beauty of the heavens, before his soul snapped back into place.

Calmly, Blaze withdrew. He rose unsteadily to his feet, allowing both Grace and Raven the luxury of movement, and breath, something neither had had in a while judging by their harrowed expressions.

He willed his feathers away, so that the glossy black wings dissolved into nothing more than an elaborate decoration across his shoulder blades, and then gave a languid stretch, straightened the clothes he'd managed to keep on and sauntered over to the cheval glass.

Blood surrounded his mouth and had dried

in smears across his chin. Blaze irritably rubbed them away. Now sated the thought of all that consumption sat foul with him. Blood, sex, and feasting on one another, what sort of deranged mentality relished such prospects? He dug his teeth into his lips until it hurt, figuring he really ought to feel bad, but the truth was he didn't feel nearly as bad as he ought. To block out his uneasiness over his lack of remorse, Blaze picked up a pot of wax and set to work coaxing his hair back into the impressive spikes his earlier shower had destroyed.

A shadow swept across the surface of the mirror so fast it only just registered on his peripheral vision. Blaze's instincts snapped to attention. He carefully scanned the room's reflection. Nothing. Nothing obvious anyway, except he could feel the presence jangling his nerve-endings.

He didn't blink. Blaze spun, and reached out a hand. For a moment, his fist formed around cool leather as the demon decloaked from the shadows inches before him. Then it vanished again, equally fast, leaving him holding nothing but air.

"Hellfire!" Raven vaulted off the bed, knocking Grace to the floor in the process. She hissed at him, but he paid her no regard. Instead he slammed into Blaze, knocking him hard up against the mirror.

"What?" Blaze gasped.

Male laughter tinkled through the ether as if it were being channelled into the room through pipes. Then the shadow rematerialized into greaves and gauntlets and leather armour. Until the only softness in the shape before him was in the form of two great black wings. Tiny red spots dotted the pinions of each feather, which retrospectively might have been specks of blood rather than markings.

Raven wrestled the demon face first into the side of the armoire.

"Still playing lapdog?"

"You." Raven released the figure with a huff. He nodded at Blaze then back-stepped a couple of paces. The male turned slowly. Eyes like black bore holes focused entirely upon Blaze.

"So it's true. The prodigal lord has returned."

"Skaa," Raven leaned slow and spoke into Blaze's ear, "the court assassin. Watch yourself."

Skaa had an arresting face, angular like Sorrow's, and similarly heavy in the eyebrow department. They threw all his other features into shadow, which perhaps was a bonus since he embodied everything the human population most feared when the word youkai passed their lips. Blaze could almost see his own demise mirrored in those soulless eyes.

Thin lips elongated into a vicious smile. "Why thank you for that beautiful introduction, Raven." Skaa bowed. "My liege." He rose again. "Shall we skip the part where you explain why the introduction was necessary given I've been assassinating folks at your behest for two centuries and get to the point of why I'm here?"

"Why are you here?" Blaze waved the assassin towards a chair. Time he started acting his rank around here or they were going to chew him up and spit him out.

Much to his astonishment the assassin actually sat.

"It's awfully quiet on the streets. Of course there was a whole lot of fuss yestereve, bleeders traipsing around the warehouse district as if it were suddenly prime real estate. Talon popping down there in person for a visit. All very jolly and amusing."

"And? The Talon followed us onto the bridge. It's no surprise if they've doubled the watch."

Raven squeezed his shoulder in silent remonstration.

"There's no watch on the bridge," Skaa said. "Not that I mentioned the bridge."

An uneasy weight settled in Blaze's stomach. The lack of a watch didn't make sense. It seemed distinctly un-Talon like, but then maybe the deranged alchemist had other ways of keeping tabs on him, a crystal ball or some other fortune-telling gimmick.

"In fact, there's barely been a whisper of Talon presence anywhere since the little fandango last night. I reckon he's found a playmate, an especially tasty one since it dragged him from his lair. Talon doesn't walk abroad without a damn good reason."

"Asha!" Her name slipped from between Blaze's lips before he thought better of it. If Talon had her... *I'm an idiot, a fucking humungous idiot.* He'd been furtling around here in safety, pretending he was a Prince and meanwhile Talon had caught her. There'd been plenty of them in pursuit and she'd been running a fever.

He shook off Raven's hold and blindly paced, oblivious to the pensive expressions of his observers. He ought to have sent out those scouts the moment he woke. Scratch that, he should never have let her go. She'd been off kettle; he'd known it, despite her best efforts to hide it.

"Asha Lemarche—what are your dealings with her?" Sorrow stood just inside the room, ahead of a second, blond demon who appeared to be snacking on a coxcomb. Skaa eyed him like a hawk would a vole, his black—no amber—irises aglow with interest.

"Doesn't anyone knock around here?" Blaze snapped. His pacing came to an abrupt halt.

Sorrow gave a shrug and closed the door. He and coxcomb boy perched on either end of the dressing table. Skaa, meanwhile, tugged off one leather gauntlet and chucked it onto the bed. "We've suffered many losses at her hands. I find your mention of her particularly disturbing, especially following your extended absence. Where've you been, Blaze? And why is Talon so interested in one of his own? And more importantly, one who's known to be utterly loyal. Talon may guard his secrets well, but even he can't mask the scent of his body. She's been his most favoured concubine for years."

"Not anymore." Blaze scrunched up a fistful of hair, surprising himself with the outburst.

But his heart was thudding like crazy. He was sorely tempted to rip a slice off someone. He contained his anger to a growl. "I have to know what's going on in there. Stop whatever that bastard's doing to her, and get her out."

The demand met with a collective indrawn breath.

"Blaze." Raven grabbed hold of his shoulders again. "She made her choice when she left, and it was the right one. She can't come here. We've been through this."

"Yes," he replied, staring the demon straight in his mismatched eyes, "we have. You need me. Without me, there is no youkai rule. The Blood Moon will wax and wane and nothing will change unless I act to initiate my reign."

"Are you saying that's the price of your cooperation?" Skaa's irises reverted to their soulless black.

Blaze held his tongue and let his silence speak for him.

Their shock rippled around the room. Youkai blood won out over their human guises.

The room seemed far more crowded with all their wings and fangs on display. Coxcomb boy gave a howl of outrage. Quickly silenced, he was pleased to note, with a hot glare.

"It's very simple. You help free the woman I love, or I do nothing. You bastards understand love, right? Or is it really all sex and no strings between you?" He rapped his fist against Raven's chest. "Any real hearts beating inside those chests?"

Maybe he'd pushed them too far. He was

taking a chance here, making the assumption he was as indispensable as Raven and Asha had come to have him believe.

The tension swelled until it threatened to implode under its own weight. Skaa slowly stood.

"Seriously—Asha Lemarche? You've chosen Talon's chief head-hunter and concubine as your mate?"

A clamour broke out among the other youkai, who suddenly all had questions for him. Blaze waited out the furore, not speaking until the room fell silent.

"Yes."

"Have you claimed her?" Sorrow's baritone sliced through the painful quiet.

"Is that any of your business?"

"It is if you expect us to honour you. I repeat, have you marked her? Is she your destined mate?"

He raised his brows as a snarl of denial left Grace's throat.

"Mate?" Blaze asked.

"Soul-mate, wife, queen."

That seemed overly dramatic. "She's the only reason I'm here with you now. We wouldn't have got anywhere near the bridge without Asha's aid."

"But did you claim her?"

"What my brother is asking is does she carry your mark?" Skaa interjected.

Blaze worried a torn piece of skin on his lip. "In essence, yes."

"Where?"

"On her palm."

"No, it can't be." Grace, who had been obsessively rubbing her hand since her first outburst launched herself straight at Blaze, her fangs bared and her tiny wings flapping so fast they made the air around them hum. "I was promised. You promised."

She went straight for his eyes, extending her talons as she dived.

Raven snatched her out of the air.

"Put her down, Raven."

In the fraction of a second it took Blaze to realise she'd actually scratched him and blood was trickling down his cheek, Skaa had already licked him clean, and coxcomb boy had flown his perch and got right up in Raven's face.

His chief guard dropped Grace and shoved her defender away, only for the fool to return with his claws raised.

"Back the hell off, Flo."

Menace radiated off Skaa. His shadow seemed to stretch out from his body, and Flo dropped to the floor gasping for breath.

"As if Blaze ever made your sibling such a promise. Raven is just doing his job. Perhaps you ought to start doing yours."

Filmy black matter seeped from Flo's mouth and nose. He rose, coughing and gasping from breath.

"Maybe he didn't, but his father did."

Blaze shrugged. He had serious memory blinkers on where his family were concerned. He couldn't even name his father.

Curiously, Skaa replicated his shrug.

"Whatever pact the former prince made is irrelevant now. He's long dead, and our law is very clear on that matter. The dead cannot impose their will upon the living. That, and if this woman is already marked, the choice is made. There's no undoing it."

"You expect us to acknowledge a human queen?" Flo snarled. He tugged his sister out of Skaa's reach before turning his venomous stare upon Blaze. "You've been missing for decades and yet you expect us still to be loyal. What chain of command did you leave in place when you vanished? None. What promise did you leave of your return? You abandoned us. Why should we even follow you?"

"Because he's our only hope," Sorrow remarked. "And all these things you list are his right. A human queen is a fair price for paving our way to Earth."

Flo snorted and turned away. He held his sister close to his body. "Assuming such a thing is possible," he muttered under his breath.

Skaa turned to Blaze, one darkling eyebrow artfully raised. "Let us be clear on this. You have our loyalty, Blaze, and we will honour your choice of queen, setting aside our grievances over her past offences against our race. In return, you will take up the mantle you've disregarded these past years and lead us across the bridge to our freedom and victory. The palace walls grow ever closer, our people want space to spread their wings and soar free. Long years we've awaited this."

"Help me free her from Talon's clutches,

and I'll lead you anywhere you like." He could be a figurehead, maybe even more than that. If he earned their respect and loyalty, perhaps he could also temper their actions on Earth, prevent the slavery the human prophets predicted. Perhaps once the initial orgy was done, he could find a way of having youkai and humans co-exist on an equal footing.

As he turned and scanned the other faces in the room, it dawned on Blaze that they were as confused by what was happening as he. They were used to his being their anchor, a stable, familiar figure driven by desires and lusts they understood. Likely, here too were the friends he'd chosen to spend his time among. Now they were all strangers, and he had to become the man...demon he'd once been.

Yet he was that demon no longer.

He'd been reborn, reinvented.

Nothing made a whole lot of sense anymore, save his need for Asha. If he thought of her, concentrated his efforts, he could sense her moods. Subdued now, he nevertheless sensed her deep down agitation. If he worked on exploring the bond, maybe it would help them pinpoint her location.

"I'll have a watch set out." Skaa stood to attention before him. "A couple of gargoyles on the cathedral roof should do it. Raven, if you could see to a few recon patrols, too."

"Consider it already done."

And then they left. All except Sorrow, who shrugged and resumed adjusting his pocket watch.

5. VIGIL

"STILL OUT HERE?"

Jaku raised his head from the cradle he'd made with his arms, in order to peer up at Talon. His master stood cloaked in shadow, in the half-open doorway to his chamber in the cathedral.

He'd donned a pair of spray-on trousers he hadn't bothered to fasten, so they sat on his slender hips just below the level of his barbed wire tattoos, the fly parted, displaying a glimpse of the golden curls beneath. As if there'd been any doubt in Jaku's mind about what had gone on over the last few hours. He'd listened to Asha's whimpers and screams, followed by a period of silence that had stretched into the early hours. The smell of sex still clung to Talon's skin. He looked tired. The skin beneath his eyes was heavily wrinkled, giving him the sunken appearance of one of Kell's acolytes. The ones who starved themselves in pursuit of inner peace, and believed the youkai lived and breathed inside them all.

He caught a glimpse of his own reflection in the brass door handle. That was one of the good things about slapping on so much paint. It covered a myriad of imperfections. Even after a night on the floor he looked damn regal.

"Is she..." he asked, afraid of the answer.

"She's resting, as you should have been. It's been a hard fight. You can count it lucky that you found her when you did, an hour longer and I'm not sure I'd have pulled her back. The demon got under her skin. His poison's gone deep. Even now, I'm not sure I'd count on a total recovery."

"But she's alive?" And not damaged beyond repair. He didn't need another death on his hands. There'd already been enough of those.

Judging by the cramp in his joints as he uncurled, he'd dozed off at some point over the last hour. The air held that pre-dawn chill the dead left behind in their wake. The streets would be clean again, and outside the cathedral walls, the sun's rays were surely streaking orange daubs across the violet night sky, but he needed to sleep. However, before he went anywhere, he needed to see Asha for himself. He didn't know why he'd trusted Talon for so long, other than it had been convenient to do so, and to never question, but now he needed proof Talon hadn't caused more damage than he'd fixed.

Talon pushed the door wide as Jaku shuffled forward. "You can come in, but don't disturb her. Sleep's a wonderful restorative."

Asha lay pale as death in Talon's sumptuously grotesque bed, the effects of the poison still evident from her scent, although at least her skin no longer had quite such a sickly shine to it. Jaku gently touched her brow. Temperature seemed normal. "What did you give her?" he asked, not expecting an answer that made any sense. Talon was a master of lying by omission.

The alchemist curled on the bed above the covers, resting on his side. "A few herbs, some sedatives, part of myself, and not just in the way you think. She needed a transfusion."

That explained the sunken shadows around Talon's eyes. A night without sleep hadn't caused that. The alchemist was used to burning the candle at both ends.

"You gave her your tainted blood?" Accusation bled into his words. "You could have called." He'd have given his willingly.

"Blaze tried to claim her," Talon continued, his voice low and sleepy. "He's been living off her energy. Likely there's still a connection we need to break if we ever want to see a full recovery. All I've really done is put some binders on the process to slow it down."

Teeth gritted, Jaku grasped Asha's palm within his own clasped hands.

"Asha, I'm so sorry." In a sense he was to

blame for this. She'd wanted to leave Blaze where they'd first found him, whereas he'd insisted on a little compassion, and only because he couldn't tolerate the thought of so much beauty going to waste. Blaze was pretty.

He sniffed. Of course he was. The youkai prince wasn't going to be an ugly bastard, was he? Well, maybe he was in his youkai form, but that wasn't going to get him anywhere amongst the City's human population.

"I knew he was bad for you. I should have acted sooner."

He should have dragged her off and sat on her the moment he realised her Blood Rain addiction had nurtured a fascination in Blaze.

Guilty tears wetted his cheeks. Jaku leaned forward and gently kissed her fingertips. "I won't let him get away with this."

"My sentiments exactly," Talon echoed. He lay sprawled upon his back. "And we won't."

Jaku homed in on the comment.

"How?"

All the reports said Blaze had crossed the bridge to his palace among the stars. No means of following him existed. A unit had tried, and ended up with wet feet for their efforts. The bodies of those who'd originally pursued Blaze onto the bridge had washed up downstream in the early hours. That being one of the many messages he'd accepted on Talon's behalf during his vigil.

"We can't do anything unless he comes out, and then he's likely to do so with the whole youkai horde at his side."

"Questions, such questions." Yawning, Talon waved them away. "Come up here. We'll worry over it when we're rested. Tired heads don't make the best plans." He patted the bed beside him. "Come."

Jaku kicked off his boots and crawled over to the space. He lay down resting his head in the crook of Talon's shoulder.

"Rest easy, Jaku, I don't forget those who attempt to steal from me, and know this, the youkai have been among us for years, and we've not yet been crushed beneath their wings. Their sympathizers in the City are dealt with. They'll find no support among the populace. Even if they march upon us at midday, we don't have to fight until we are ready. We'll have our revenge. But it will be well planned revenge, not an ill-conceived backlash in the heat of rage. You must let your anger simmer down and burn cold. The demons won't rule us."

DEMON RULE. It wasn't really something Blaze wanted to think about.

Having finally managed to fix his hair to perfection and reapply the kohl around his eyes, Blaze slumped onto the ocean-sized bed in his suite and gave a sigh. "Is there an outside in this place? I could really use some air."

He could really use a job too, something to take his mind off what he'd agreed to and what nightmares Talon was busy subjugating Asha to. She'd been agitated, and although she was calm again now he wasn't at all reassured over her safety. That bastard had been abusing her for years, poisoning her, and mentally as well as physically screwing her. He'd give a lot of money to be able to throw a punch or two in Talon's direction and leave him swallowing teeth. Instead he was left thumping a pillow because his subjects didn't trust him not to renege on their deal and fly off.

As if he were that dumb.

He might not know much at the minute but he did have some concept of his limitations, and taking on Talon single-handed was downright stupid unless he wanted to end up as someone's minced dinner.

"Hey," he prompted. "That was a question?"

"Sure, I heard you." Sorrow whistled through his teeth. "It's just there isn't much of an outside. There's the Queen's Gardens. They're dome covered, but nah—not a good idea. Save your strength."

"One measly garden, that's it? Crap palace. Aren't there any balconies?"

Sorrow removed his spectacles and took a cleaning cloth to the lenses. "I thought you wanted room to pace."

"No. I want to do."

Blaze propped himself up and watched the action of applying the cloth to the lenses.

"Do you actually need those?" He hadn't considered demons having any sort of disability before.

"I can spot a rat from forty yards away. It's

close up I'm not so good, which makes mending laborious," Sorrow replied. The bits of his pocket watch were spread across the floor again, along with pieces of something else that might have been a compass. Sorrow gathered them up, sliding the cogs and pins into various pockets. "Nearest balcony is through there."

Blaze followed his nod to a latticework screen he'd taken for a decorative piece of nonsense. There were no visible catches or handles with which to open it. Sorrow appeared at his shoulder.

"You have to stick your finger in here and give it a bit of a twist."

Since Sorrow had accomplished the action, Blaze passed over the opportunity for practice.

"You didn't have to follow."

"You're joking. Raven will sauté me if you get so much as a scratch. Can't risk an aerial attack."

"You're not just tagging along in case I break my parole?"

Sorrow gave him a thoughtful look. "I don't think you're going anywhere, but it pays to be safe, and I mean that in terms of avoiding attack rather than you hatching an escape plan." He pressed the tip of his tongue to his upper lip then patted Blaze upon the shoulder. "I'm not going to pretend I understand, but I can see the separation is cutting you up."

"Thanks," Blaze vaguely mumbled.

"You might want to let me lead." Sorrow shuffled past him.

"Surely it's safe up here? Raven said we'd be out of Talon's reach here."

Sorrow stopped short, having moved no more than two paces. "Well, yeah, that's technically true. Only we've moved since then. You might not be as vulnerable as you were down in the city, but you're not entirely out of reach. I'm sure Talon could move a mountain if he put his mind to it. Plus, there are plenty of stalkers inside the castle."

That was it. He'd had enough of talking in circles.

"What stalkers? And we've moved where exactly?" And how? "Is this place on wheels?" He shoved his way past Sorrow and strode out onto the balcony. It seemed normal enough at first. Stars twinkling in the heavens. Space as inky and vast as ever. Of course the balcony wasn't entirely normal, but it didn't shock him in the way the living flames that composed the Division Bridge had. Here the filigree scrollwork wasn't fiery, but composed of liquid metal. Bemused, he stuck his hand into it and watched the pattern flow around him, producing a sensation similar to pins and needles. It was only when he looked up that his sanity took a rain check and his lunch decided it would have been better to say indoors.

The Old City hung above him, streets and houses clearly discernible. The Eyrie hung down like an enormous stalactite, the roof of the cathedral formed another point. Even the odd figure could be seen walking about.

"Are we upside down, or are they?" he

asked, his fingers forming claws around the balustrade.

Sorrow shrugged. "Us. Ready to go in again?"

Blaze nodded. "I think I'm going to puke." And since he wasn't at all sure in which direction gravity was working, going inside to do it seemed the best option.

THERE WERE NO lights in Talon's chamber, but Jaku woke knowing it was fully daylight. Talon still lay beside him, the rise and fall of his chest rapid against his back. He reached out an arm and found the space in which Asha had lain empty. Instantly alert, heart beating nineteen to the dozen, Jaku rolled over to wake Talon, only to find Asha straddled over his master's hips. He reached out, but stopped short of touching her. She looked so perfect it made his heart bleed. Her eyes were closed, her delicate features suffused with pleasure as her body rocked. She'd stripped virtually naked, except for a black bodice that cinched her waist and crested the lower swell of her breasts.

They were locked together, perfectly complimenting one another, both relaxed, both clearly caught up in the moment of passion. Talon's eyes were only open a tiny fraction, his sensual lips drawn into a smile.

Hurt grabbed Jaku in the pit of his stomach. He scrambled back an inch or two, but couldn't look away.

Finally seeing them together was worse than he'd ever imagined. They fit in a way he and Talon didn't.

Asha rocked harder and let out an indulgent groan. She collapsed forward onto Talon's chest and rubbed her cheek against him then set to sucking his nipples.

Talon responded by lifting an arm to wrap around her.

Jaku did a double take. Silvered images of the moon in all its phases were inked onto the skin on the inside of Talon's forearm. The full moon symbol had turned silvery-red. It was here—the Blood Moon had arrived.

He rolled sideways and lurched off the bed. Oblivious to the calls of chastisement for leaving open every door, he fled through the network of chambers and passages into the vast open nave of the cathedral. Through the rose window above the main entrance he caught a glimpse of the sky, no longer blue, but a muggy orange-brown, like the dregs at the bottom of a beer cask. The time had come. He raced outside to stand in the centre of the deserted plaza overlooking the canal. They had a few hours perhaps before the youkai made their assault. He needed to motivate the troops before the sun, now a nondescript lighter disk barely discernible from the background colour of the sky, disappeared altogether.

Jaku turned southwest towards the direction of the Division Bridge, although the bridge itself was too far off to see, even if the view hadn't been impeded by houses. A bleak dot hung in the sky above the Heights. He stared at it, hand shielding his gaze, tried squinting, but couldn't quite bring it into proper focus.

"The youkai palace."

He turned to find Ouran beside him, also squinting up at the dot.

"It appeared forty minutes ago. Someone is informing Talon now. They've also sent a delegation to watch our movements."

"Youkai?" His desperate hope that they were talking about winged beasties and not more human sympathisers seeped into his question.

"If they are, they're not like any youkai I've ever seen. They're grey. Only reason we spotted them is because we saw them arrive. Otherwise—" he shrugged "—they blend in."

They went back inside to find Talon had risen. He'd thrown a long red robe on over a pair of black brocade trousers. Asha sat on a padded cushion at his feet, gorgeous in a cloud of red and black fabric. Her make-up had been reapplied, by Talon he suspected. Certainly not by her, since her eyes were completely vacant.

"Jaku—" Talon hooked one long leg over the top of the other, "—if you'd be so kind as to lead a delegation up onto the roof to address our visitors. I think I'd like a word or two with them."

"Should I invite them to breakfast?"

"No need, but you can serve them a rent notice if they don't remove themselves from my roof. I can't abide squatters."

6. GRUB'S UP

"Only a fool mistakes a youkai grub for a demon child.
Though from such grubs winged adults grow."
--Vesper Canon. Wicked Times. Chapter 10.

HIS STOMACH HAVING recovered from the hellish mind fuck of stepping outside, Blaze decided it was time to make an effort to find out what was going on. Leaders led. They didn't sit on their backsides getting all grouchy and watching their muscles turn to mush. Memory or not, he had to face the youkai aristocracy at some point. It might as well be now. Nobody seemed concerned about the opinions of the rabble, which wasn't so very different to the world he was used to. Politicians and the city leaders rarely ventured into the Birdcage. Most of them rarely set foot outside the Heights, which is how Talon managed to have such a stranglehold on everything north of the river.

Considering how much time Sorrow spent with his nose in his watch mechanism it would have been easy to slide out of the room, but hey, his survival instinct was still alive and kicking.

"Let's go for a walk," Blaze announced, shrugging on his leather jacket.

"That's not such a—"

"It wasn't a request. The only reason you're invited is because you know where you're going."

Sorrow stood immediately. He ran his tongue over his surprisingly white teeth.

"Where to?" Curiously, he didn't seem overly concerned about dissuading him, but then maybe he'd been waiting for Blaze to show some steel.

"Business centre, bar, throne room, wherever the central hub of power is."

"There's not a flicker of recollection in there, is there?"

There wasn't, but in all fairness that's the way it was. There was no point dwelling on it any longer. He'd just have to engage in some spectacular bluffing and stomach a sharp learning curve.

"Not a teeny tiny smidgen."

"Watch it."

A broad grin stretched across Sorrow's narrow face giving him a distinctly cadaverous look.

"I like you when you get all shirty. Reminds me just what a pissy bugger you can be. All right, let's go. Just warn me before you plan to fuck anyone, okay."

"Was that fuck or fuck with?"

Sorrow's grin morphed into a low chuckle.

"With you, I'm not so sure there's a difference." He patted Blaze upon the shoulder before strolling over to the bed and pulling Blaze's gun from beneath the pillow. "I'm assuming since you were carrying it, you know how to fire this thing."

"Point and pull. Is this entirely necessary to walk down the corridor?"

"Yeah."

"Succinct bastard, aren't you?" Blaze checked the barrel. The gun had been cleaned and reloaded. "What about my knife?"

"Blunt as shit. Here, you can take this." Sorrow snatched a long wavy bladed kris off the wall and offered up the hilt. The cold steel glinted in the torch-light and elaborate scrollwork which seemed to contain a form of script decorated the bottom six inches of the shaft. "Even if I'm going to pray you don't need to use that."

"Ye of little faith."

"Sword play was never your thing, and that beauty never sat easy within your palm, but you asked, so there it is, and we'll see what may."

Interesting, since the pistol-shaped grip sat comfortably in his palm, and the whole blade gave him a curious tingly thrill just from holding it. The kris felt more right than anything else around here.

THE CORRIDOR WAS eerily quiet and every footstep echoed like a drum roll. Blaze cringed over every movement. His tension wasn't helped by Sorrow's nervousness. The demon's head constantly moved to check all three hundred and sixty degrees around them.

"What are you looking for?"

Sorrow shook his head. "It's best to stay alert. You never know what's lurking, and I don't like surprises."

"Not overly fond of surprises either, Blaze gave a quick nod. Besides, watchfulness had the secondary benefit of allowing him to digest his surroundings. He'd expected typical castle décor, windy stone corridors, exposed brickwork, stone steps, guard rooms, and maybe even a sleeping princess straight out of a storybook at the top of one long forgotten tower. Maybe those things were true of human castles. Youkai castles apparently followed different design rules. For starters no one seemed to differentiate between the walls, floor, and ceiling. They were all stone and all formed not of bricks but huge slabs of granite, which looked like they'd been hewn into meaty slices by a colossal bread knife. There was a certain similarity between them and the rock hewn walls in the Hall of Ancients on top of the Eyrie. However, those walls had definitely been rock, whereas these—Blaze wasn't so sure. The texture felt fleshy, organic, not rigid, a fact made particularly disturbing by the proliferation of carved imps over every surface, underfoot, overhead, swinging from the wall sconces and staring at them with horribly realistic reflective eyes. As for what the leering little buggers were up to, most of it was best forgotten. The remainder was plain old lewd or revolting.

"Someone has a nice healthy obsession, I see."

"Had. The whole castle's designed by the same person. He wove everything including his last breath into the making of this place."

"My father?" Blaze asked, realising he still didn't have a name with which to honour the old man. Why had no one mentioned his mother yet?

"Yeah. Seems weird to be telling you all this when you're the one who told me."

"So, is there a purpose to it, or is it really pure aesthetics?"

"They're your eyes and ears is what I've heard. Some say you've greater command of them than that. But then some say your father wove the entire castle to protect you, while others maintain that after five cycles of time he was barking mad and simply longed for another state of being. The castle is what he chose."

"Implying that he is the castle?" Blaze chewed over the notion a moment. The place certainly gave the impression of sentience. Possibly that was down to all the movement and the flowing nature of the designs. Maybe it was something more.

"The further they travelled away from his chamber, the thicker the darkness closing in on them seemed to grow and the more the skin at the back of his neck prickled.

"Is there a torch shortage?" Wall sconces were plentiful, but only one in every six or so held a torch.

"You can blame my brother for that. You can't shadow walk without shadows." Sorrow snapped to attention, his shoulders raised. "Keep moving." He wrapped an arm around Blaze's back and ushered him forward.

"What is it?"

"Nothing. Not yet. Don't look." He stopped Blaze from turning his head. "Keep quiet and keep walking, but don't run unless I tell you. A stampede is only going to attract them."

"They managed two, perhaps three hundred yards without any hint of danger beyond Sorrow's soft insistence that they keep moving, during which time Blaze grew increasingly tense. A sour taste filled his mouth and every minute change in air temperature registered on his skin. Only after they'd turned a corner and stumbled down four flights of stairs did his senses jump like he'd been struck by lightning. He couldn't help it. Blaze swivelled around. Nothing behind him besides the maw of the stairwell, and nothing but Sorrow ahead of him.

"Except—hell's mercy—no, that wasn't true. There was something... Yes, definitely, there it was again. The wall to his right bulged slightly, like something had been pressed against a flexible skin and then withdrawn. He watched the form appear again further along the corridor; the outline of a limb, the elongated shape of a skull, and then a face, and the bloated swell of a torso.

"What in the abyss is that?"

"Shh! Shut up." Sorrow grabbed him by the shoulder and forced him into a march.

On the periphery of his vision, Blaze saw a half-dozen more figures appear, and each time they appeared the wall seemed a little more elastic.

"They're not a problem. They can't do anything to us from inside the wall."

They were a problem. Full heads and shoulders were lurching at him from out of the ceiling, arms stretching out of the ground and waving like lady's fingers.

Demon faces, he realised, only with bulging fish-like eyes and flat protruding foreheads that gave way to a ridge of bony plates over the skull and down the length of the spine.

"How do they get out? They can't get out, can they?"

"Only through a crack."

Like the split in the stonework before them where one of the wall sconces had been ripped free of the wall.

Blaze didn't wait for a prompt. He leapt past the gash, then spun around with the pistol in his hand and fired.

The bullet hit the creature in the dead centre of its chest as it slithered through the crack, provoking a cry of outrage, before it dropped and two hundred pounds of wet meat crashed to the floor.

"Now you've done it," Sorrow cursed. "Run."

They hurtled along the stretch of corridor, following hairpin bends up a ramp-like ascent. Blaze glanced back over his shoulder. The whole floor rippled as a seething, oily mass swept towards them. If it reached them, it would swarm over them like an army of ants, only with infinitely more vicious bites. The thing was already gaining on them.

Blaze picked up his pace, only to have to slow down several strides later as the corridor ended in a set of solid brass doors.

Sorrow began fumbling about in his pocket for a key.

"Couldn't you have had that ready?"

"Couldn't you have held off from alerting them?"

"Well maybe if you told me what the fuck they are."

"They're grubs. They're larvae, okay?"

"Huh?" Like he was supposed to remember what they were. Larvae? "Like maggots?"

"Us. They're us. Or some of them will be."

"Blaze drew his kris. Okay, reality timeout. No way was he in anyway related to these things, with their dead eyes and sucker-like mouths ringed with razor sharp teeth. They were... Frankly, they were gross. And way, way too close.

The muscles in his legs began to spasm in protest, and a crick formed in his neck.

"Get that damn key in the lock."

"Done it." The double doors swung inwards, but too late. The front runners jumped, propelling themselves forward on long limber legs.

Blaze reduced the first to cinders before it came within a foot of his weapon. He didn't think about it. It just happened.

The ash blew into his eyes, leaving him blinking and squinting as the second grub bowled Sorrow off his feet and fell with him so they both went tumbling into the room beyond. Deciding action was a better alternative to waiting for more of them to arrive; Blaze snatched the key from the lock and dived through the double doors. He slammed them closed quickly.

A series of hefty thuds bowed the metal as he turned the key. Now to help Sorrow, who was on the ground wrestling with the thing.

Blaze wasn't sure where they'd ended up. He wasn't sure he cared for the extra lighting either, since it exposed the grub in all its grotesque glory. Mottled grey skin covered a predominantly humanoid form, except there was no neck as such, only a thicker protuberance where the head sat. Darn thing looked exactly like an oversized grub with limbs and attitude.

The gun didn't seem a good option given how well the beast was entwined around Sorrow's form. Instead, he stabbed down with the kris, piercing its flesh near the shoulder, causing it to scream and rocket sideways. Blaze followed its spindly dance across the marble floor, and then shot it through the head at close range.

He pulled the trigger again once it stopped dancing just to make sure, then hurried over to Sorrow.

"You okay?" he asked as Sorrow scrambled to his feet. When he stood, he did so with his hand clamped across his upper thigh.

"I've had worse."

"It bit you?"

"Yeah." He glanced down at his hand and grimaced. Blood began to leak around the edge of his palm and trickled down his leg.

"Is the wound clean?"

"As clean as bites normally are. Hell. Shit." Sorrow sagged against the wall, staying mostly upright.

"Here." Blaze stuck out his wrist. "I feel responsible. It was kind of my fault."

Sorrow shook his head and began to laugh. "You're offering me... It's all right, thanks. I'll limp." He unfastened his sword from its binding around his waist and leant his weight on the scabbard.

Blaze watched him with his eyebrows raised. Considering the size of the wound, it had to be causing a hell of a lot of pain.

"Is there something wrong with my blood?"

"Yeah, I don't want you sneaking a glimpse inside my head whenever you feel like it. And I don't care for the obligation that goes with such a gift."

"Raven—"

"Raven's different. You and he have always been close."

"But if we encounter any more of those things...the grubs. What then?"

Sorrow slowly shook his head. Each whooshing of his breath seemed to contain his unspoken screams of pain.

"We won't. They haven't found a way into the walls in this part of the castle yet. Let's go. We're not far from the throne room now."

They continued on, passing through a series of bare stone antechambers. Slowly elements of furniture crept in. In one room, the left hand wall gave way to a balcony. Blaze stretched over to take a look at the land below, which appeared to be draped in vines and plants bearing enormous flowers.

"What did you mean when you said the grubs were us? That they're our children?"

"That's the Queen's Garden," Sorrow explained, as he leaned heavily on the iron balustrade beside Blaze. "And no, they're not children. A grub is a very different thing to a demon child. A grub will eventually become a worker or a foot solider. A demon child... a demon child is a blessing you won't understand until you have your memory back. They are one of the rarest things." Both his voice and his expression took on a dreamy quality as he spoke, as if the mere thought filled him with radiance and left him blessed.

"So the grubs are what the lower castes become. Why aren't they kept in check?"

"By all means, try and calm them with your authoritarian voice. They don't recognise anything but food and force, Blaze. Consider one dilemma at a time. Focus on the Blood Moon for now and save the pest control issues for a rainy day."

"Seemed there were more issues than one to dwell upon. The scent of iron caught in Blaze's nostrils. He glanced at the marble floor and saw the widening pool of blood around Sorrow's foot. Blaze knelt and folded his fingers around Sorrow calf.

"If you won't let me heal you, then at least let me bind this properly." He peeled Sorrow's sticky fingers away from the wound. Some of his blood had begun to clot, but there was a groove of flesh missing from Sorrow's thigh at the centre of the bite. Not for the last time, he wished Asha were on hand. She'd have known exactly how to treat such a wound. There'd have been painkillers and sterile water, and a needle and thread to close the gash. Not to mention sewing skills. He wasn't sure he even knew how to tie a knot in the end of the thread. Not that he had any.

Sorrow winced as he prodded. Damn if this wasn't ridiculous. Blaze pressed his lips together in thought, then took a chance on a violent reaction and licked the wound clean. He hadn't done anything Sorrow had expressly said he ought not to. There wasn't any of his blood involved, just a bit of saliva. Enough, as it turned out, to nicely seal the wound.

Sorrow ground his teeth a bit, but didn't, Blaze noted, do anything to stop him. Actually, he had a nice grin on his face when Blaze finally rose to his feet.

"All better." Blaze's lips curled into a triumphant smile. "You can thank me any time you like."

An aggravated rumble up ahead drowned out Sorrow's reply. His expression remained rueful.

"Trouble?" Blaze wondered.

"More than likely. That's the Audience Chamber."

Numerous individuals were trying to push their way into the already overcrowded hall when they arrived. Blaze started towards the door only for Sorrow to put an arm in front of his chest.

"This might not be the best time."

"There'll never be a good time. What do you suggest? That I go back to my room and wait for someone to report what all the fuss is? I'd rather find out for myself." He pushed Sorrow's arm aside. "By all means defend my back, but don't cosset me. And let's be realistic, if I want these folks to follow me into battle against Talon, then I owe them an appearance at least. They need to know I'm here."

Sorrow shot him a look that said welcome back, and moved into a defensive position behind him.

7. GA, GA, GARGOYLE

BLAZE SHOVED HIS way through the crowd, ruffling feathers and plucking a few from some stubborn folks who couldn't take a hint. An enormous red winged fool turned on him, claws raised, but he backed down the moment recognition hit.

"My liege." He dropped to one knee. "My sincere and everlasting apologies."

Okay, that was weird and several levels of freaky and humiliating all at once. Yet rather cool. Blaze stifled a lunatic grin and made do with a nod of acknowledgement. He sidestepped to go around the demon, only to find a pathway had magically opened before him, the whisper of his presence having spread. The front row of those lining the route bowed, or knelt as he past. One individual with wings like those of a gull splayed himself full length upon the floor.

Somewhat overawed by the demonstration, Blaze hurried forward. He didn't deserve their loyalty yet, having done nothing to earn it. The prince they owed fealty to was a different man—demon. He was just a boy, who'd been dragged from the Birdcage a few days ago and who had no idea how to lead an army. He knew naught of strategy and only the rudiments of assault. Not that he had much taste for facing Talon in a pitched battle, willingly or otherwise.

Blaze's gratified high soon faded. Not everybody proved quite so willing to bow. A group of dissidents slid away en mass rather than acknowledge fealty.

"More rainy day pursuits?" he remarked to Sorrow.

A deep grimace etched lines into the demon's face. "Flay, etcetera? They won't act. That's not to say they're not trouble. Doesn't matter how well you rule, there'll always be opposition and malcontents."

Considering his lengthy absence and the serious larvae problem, he could hardly blame their malcontent.

His gaze landed on Skaa standing at the front of the vast hall; the assassin's black ensemble swaddled his form, stealing light from his surroundings. He stood upon the steps leading to the dais upon which an enormous black iron throne stood. The vast structure looked about as comfortable as a sitting on a spike, despite the cushioned base. Twisted iron thorns rose to a height of eighteen feet, forming a latticework upon which were hung an assortment of crystals and other less wholesome things. He had a sneaking suspicion one of two of them might be eyeballs. Real roses, with blooms the colours of burning embers were twined around the bottom six feet of metal. Imposing and oppressive, he bowed his head, afraid to look too long upon the structure for fear of being overwhelmed by the magnitude of the mission he'd agreed to.

Was one woman worth this? How the hell did he keep a bunch of demons in check?

Skaa bowed his head as Blaze climbed the dais steps.

"I'm glad to see you've ventured among us. They needed to see you. They're eager for your touch." His gaze flicked briefly to the figure still lying prone on the floor before returning to Blaze's face.

"Any news from outside?"

The assassin ran his tongue over his impressively sharp teeth. "There has been a minor incident. I was on my way to you."

Like hell he was.

"I was fact gathering first. It seemed wiser to go to you with the whole story rather than half of one."

"Of course. Then go gather."

"Ah! I think they are coming to us."

From the door through which Blaze had entered came a large cart, pulled by four hulking brutes. Foot soldiers, he thought. They reminded him of the youkai he'd seen down in the City. Having dragged the cart full of what appeared to be granite rubble to the foot of the dais, they tipped it up, scattering the pile of rocks across the marble floor.

"Idiots." Skaa shooed them off, and began picking amongst the bits of stone. Blaze followed him down to the lower step. A large boulder lay before him. It blinked. He did a double take, and then sought confirmation of his sight from Sorrow, who gave a tiny incline of his head.

Blaze squatted down on the steps, and gave the boulder a poke. Okay, it was definitely a head. The damn thing groaned as it rolled over. The nose was missing, as too were an ear and an eye, and a huge crack ran diagonally across the thing's cranium.

"What is—"

"They're the gargoyles I posted." Skaa returned to his side. "It seems they were spotted."

Gargoyles were living statues. Blaze took a deep breath, and wondered whether to log them alongside Wisht Hounds as animals or on an equal footing with humans and the youkai.

"Since when was having your spies sent back to you in pieces a minor incident? Can we find out what happened? Discover if Asha's all right?"

Skaa's hand flicked up off his knee, his fingers splayed in warning.

Blaze gave him an exasperated growl. "Fine. Are you going to dispel the horde or shall we just ask them all to stick their fingers in their ears and hum? They'll find out about Asha sooner or later, seems pointless hiding it, when she's going to be my queen."

Skaa lowered his hand. "Of course. You're right. They will learn of it soon enough, but there's no need to give them ammunition against you. The situation here is delicate, Blaze. You've been missing a long time."

Agreed. It wasn't that he didn't believe Raven when he said he was loved by his people, but Raven hadn't taken into account his rather long sojourn in the world below. Of course people were tetchy. Naturally they had questions, most of which he couldn't provide decent answers for.

One pertinent point did strike him. "Who's been in command in my absence?"

"I have." Skaa flashed him a worrying smile.

"Should I fear a rebellion?" He held his steward's gaze until Skaa gave the tiniest shake of his head.

"I gave you my pledge earlier. Ascendancy transcends petty internal politics. I might envy your throne, but I can't catapult us back to our rightful place."

Blaze accepted the explanation with a nod. "I'll remind you of that when you stab me in the back."

Amusement flashed across Skaa's stern features, briefly tugging the edges of his thin lips upwards.

"Should I opt to engage in regicide, you won't know about it until it's too late." The shadows around Skaa seemed to coalesce as he spoke, transforming what might have been idle banter into a potential threat, just as his smile took on a malevolent twist.

They eyed one another cautiously, until Raven's arrival shattered the air of tension.

"I've brought some glue," he announced. "I heard they'd arrived back from Flo. He and Grace are on bridge watch. What's going on here?" He slapped Blaze across the back, before sagging onto his knees to inspect the broken gargoyle. "Damn hard to kill gargoyles. Shame they've never made very good frontline troops. They just sink into depression and start writing poetry."

"You mean they don't die from being broken up like this." Blaze turned his head from side to side, hardly able to comprehend being shattered into so many pieces and still living. In a similar position he'd wish for death. Who the hell wanted to be looking at their testicles separated from their body by ten feet of marble tiling? Poor sods.

"Nah," Skaa replied. "You have to pretty much powder them." He stuck his hand out towards Raven. "Pass the glue."

"Do you reckon they've sent the lot back?" Sorrow asked, as he began stacking up a pile of fingers.

Skaa squeezed out a large dollop of glue and pieced together a section of jaw. "I'm not planning on whiling away my time finding out. Let's stick to the essentials here. There, that should do it." The newly glued fragments slid into place, neatly repairing the gargoyle's lower jaw, except for a minor chip on the chin.

"Right up, Grruf, what happened?"

The stone head screamed.

Blaze clamped his hands over his ears. The act barely deadened the shriek that made the walls and his ears vibrate.

"Grruf! Shut the fuck up, will you." Skaa's grip tightened on the stone head, which kept on screaming.

"Lift him onto the throne," Blaze insisted.

"Are you crazy?" The way Raven's brows furrowed suggested he was exactly that.

"It's just a seat and a damned uncomfortable looking one at that. Besides, I'm sick of looking at my feet, and I'm thinking a bit of eye contact might help."

"Good point. But not the throne."

"There's a table to the right. Raven, you help me carry him."

Bemused, despite the ear pain, Blaze watched the two demons manoeuvre the stone head onto a side table clearly intended to house a dish of appetisers not a granite block. It gave an ominous creak as they set down the head, but held.

"Right." Blaze got onto his knees in order to be eyelevel with the gargoyle. "Quit wailing, and I'll assign a team to get you fixed, but first I need to know what happened over at the cathedral. Did Talon do this? Did you see Asha?"

"Maybe one question at a time," Sorrow remarked. "Don't want to overburden it."

The granite eyes stopped rolling and the

beheaded creature actually managed a look of contrition. "I apologise, my liege, and thank you."

They breathed a unanimous sigh of relief.

"I don't know how he knew we were up there, but he sent a group up. As soon as they realised the only damage they were doing was to their weapons they traipsed back down again. Next thing we know, the floor's rising up so fast we didn't have time to blink, let alone flex the wings. He sunk us right through the roof."

"Stylish," remarked Skaa.

Blaze frowned. "Well, that explains why you're in bits. There are two of you here, right?" He quickly surveyed the rubble, but if there was another head amongst it, it was broken beyond immediate recognition.

"Grym," Skaa clarified.

"So what did Talon say? I assume he had you scooped up and ferried back here for a reason?"

Grruf's lips moved for several seconds before his voice began to work in synch. "He invites you to parley, my prince, and offers the Lady Asha as a gesture of good faith for your attendance."

Blaze sat back on his haunches and covered his mouth with his hand. "He expects me to walk into his stronghold after the stunt he pulled on my last visit?"

The gargoyle managed to look offended he'd even consider passing on such a message. "Nay, indeed he suggested you met on neutral ground of your choosing, the warehouse district near the Division Bridge being given as a potential location."

Blaze pushed onto his feet. He paced still rubbing his jaw, torn between his desire to have Asha safely at his side and his mistrust of Talon. "What you think?" he asked, catching Raven's eye.

"I don't know. I don't trust him."

"That's a given." Talon was bound to have something planned. Asking for talks was tantamount to admitting having reached a stalemate, if not plain admitting defeat. Bastard had something up his sleeve.

"And Asha, did you see her? How was she?"

"Only a glimpse, assuming she was the lady who sat at his feet. She seemed well, if subdued."

Subdued. He once seen Asha in that state himself, when she'd been in the midst of a Blood Rain high. He sincerely hoped it was an act intended to put Talon off his guard and not actual poisoning.

"Any other rules to this gathering I should know about?"

"Just that he requests you bring only a small personal guard to avoid raising alarm in the city and that he will do likewise. The time should be set for dusk tonight to avoid the fullness of the moon."

"It's too dangerous." Skaa slapped his open palm down on the table beside the head, causing the wood to give another ominous creak.

"The hell it is, Skaa. I need her back."

The assassin stared him down.

"You're not strong enough yet. The transformation's not complete. Talon knows it. It's why he wants the meeting so soon."

"Fuck the damn moon. It's nothing but a signpost. We're going to this meeting. Sorrow, take a group out and scout the warehouses. Once you've found somewhere appropriate, have a message sent over to the cathedral. We agree to the meeting at dusk."

Despite the decisiveness of his actions, Sorrow stood a moment in hesitation. He slid a pensive glance towards his brother.

"Ahem," Blaze interjected.

Slowly, Sorrow bowed his head. "Yes, of course."

"Pits of Hades. You'll regret this." Skaa gave an outraged tut. "If we're genuinely doing this then let us at least pick wisely. Wait up there, brother. I'd best come too."

The pair left together.

Blaze sucked in a deep breath, and dearly wished he could stick his head in a vat full of sand. While the crowd of nobles hadn't been silent during the last few moments, they'd certainly been paying attention to the exchange, and looked like they were awaiting an announcement.

"Soon," he mouthed to himself. It wasn't as if he had an obligation to explain. Having caught the sight of the male who'd previously splayed himself flat, Blaze beckoned him over. "There are two gargoyles here. See that they're fixed." He handed him the tube of glue Skaa had left behind, then caught Raven's eye. "We need to talk, somewhere private?"

"Prince's Sanctuary. Behind the throne."

Perfect. Blaze dragged his chief guard to the rear of the dais.

The walls of the Prince's Sanctuary glinted gold, the radiance almost too bright to look upon, but then the whole palace was overkill. Above the ocean of gold, lay panels of verdant green and topaz blue, the latter comprised of millions of tiny square tiles. Overlaid upon the background, and similarly fashioned, were six huge rainbow-hued birds. Blaze shoved Raven up against the nearest wall as soon as they were safely out of sight.

"Is there a reason why you're all handing me the bits of this puzzle one piece at a time? Can we not just have a definitive, this-is-what-the-fuck-is-going-on conversation and be done with it. One minute I'm transformed, the next, we're not quite there yet. So talk, tell me what the fuck it is I'm not being told."

The guy had the audacity to look shocked. He spluttered a moment, lips flapping but no words coming out, his cheeks becoming blotched, a sure sign of conspiratorial guilt.

Blaze clucked in annoyance and stared down at his feet. The floor consisted of a mosaic phoenix set within an oval of flames. Another reference to the Burning Prince he'd agreed to become, he supposed. However, it was only through looking down at the bird that he realised Raven's lack of response was due to oxygen deprivation. He'd lifted the other demon clean off his feet.

Hell, he'd grown strong. Hadn't even realised it, and he hadn't gained any bulk. He was still as wiry as he'd ever been. After dropping Raven back onto his feet, Blaze gave an uncomfortable shrug in lieu of an apology and turned his back to mask his embarrassment.

Raven coughed a moment or two and then walked around to Blaze's fore, still rubbing his neck. A dark red V ringed the underside of his jaw, but the colour was already fading from the edges.

"You always did have a nasty grip." He lowered his hand. "I'm not deliberately hiding things, Blaze, it's more a case of you never asked. I don't know what you do know and what you don't. And I'm piecing this stuff together myself. Never bothered with Kell's Prophecy you see. Lunatic human drivel. Couldn't see the point."

"And this is about that?"

A brief shake of his head followed. "No, not exactly. Only partially." Raven rested his arse on the flimsy little bench to the right of the door.

Blaze looked around for somewhere to sit, but the chamber was seriously lacking in the furniture department.

"Why is it so sodding bare in here? T'aint much of a sanctuary without a few home comforts."

Raven splayed his hands. He had his elbows

rested upon his knees. "It's the way you used to like it."

"Guess I wasn't much for sitting down." Unfortunately, he had the impression what was coming required a seated position, otherwise he'd end up wearing a groove in the tiles with his pacing. Blaze crossed his legs and hunkered down on the floor, prompting a chuckle from Raven.

"Actually, you used to hunch down right about there."

A quick look told him 'there' was right over the phoenix's heart, maybe there was even a bit of bottom-shaped wear in the tiles.

"So, tell me. If we're going to meet with Talon, I need to know this stuff, right? What's this mark about that I've inflicted upon Asha? Why the sudden insistence that she's my Queen?"

And why Queen for that matter? Shouldn't it make her his princess, if his title was only prince?

Having rubbed a few circles into the sides of his throat, Raven clapped his hands together. "You realise Skaa or Sorrow would probably give you a better explanation."

"And they'd leave out anything they thought might jeopardize the arrangement, whereas you, my friend, are going to tell me the whole, right?" He flashed him a grin. Curious how he'd kind of accepted Raven's friendship while he remained wary of the others. But then Raven had been down in the City with him and had watched his back, front, and sides. They'd been swapping a fair amount of blood, too. He imagined that created a bit of a bond.

Raven made an odd clacking noise with his teeth. "You're not going to like all of it. Thing is Blaze, regardless, it's too late to stop it. Queen because she's your chosen mate, your soul mate, and I mean it in a more literal way than you're perhaps used to from the bleeders." He paused as if gathering his thoughts. "It's an old, old practice. You rarely see it amongst us anymore, we're too jealous of our power to risk sharing, even with someone we've bound ourselves to for centuries. Especially the females, because it leaves them weakened. And even then it only ever occurred amongst the aristocracy. It was a way of assuring allegiances."

"Kind of like an exchange of hostages?"

"No... Yes... Kind of, except more complicated. You've literally mated your souls."

Blaze's eyebrows shot upwards. Human philosophers were still debating the soul's actual existence but apparently the youkai had been marrying them for aeons.

"Or more accurately, Asha's given one of hers into your keeping."

"Whoa, hold up!" Blaze raised his hand for a pause. Philosophy and the nature of being weren't two of his hot topics at the best of times, but according to everything he'd ever heard, the theory progressed along the lines of one person, one soul.

"We each have two souls." Raven nodded his head as if that were established fact.

Blaze shook his head in turn.

"Okay, just accept it for the minute. Once the mating process between you and Asha is complete, you'll have three. The triumvirate is strong, incredibly strong. It'll elevate you way above the level of any other youkai noble or bleeder. You might consider it the final step in your transformation. That's what Skaa was getting at. He wants you mated. It's the method by which Blaze Makaresh transforms into the Burning Prince, the leader whose rise will give us back the Earth. So of course he wants it, but that necessitates us having Asha, and hence putting you at risk."

It took a moment or two to tumble over the facts in his head. He couldn't ever recall coming across the notion of being having more than one soul. Three seemed overkill somehow.

"So ultimately it's my taking a mate that's important, not the Blood Moon?"

"I think the two events are kind of seen to coincide."

"Right. And I'm guessing Asha and I need to properly cement the bond between us. Get married or something," he said dubiously. "Assuming she even agrees."

"Precisely. She hasn't released her soul to you yet."

"And you think Talon knows this and that's why he's using her as a carrot?"

Raven shrugged. "Wouldn't want to hazard a guess on that one. I've never been able to figure that bastard out. But you can bet he'll want his pound of flesh at this meeting. No way on fucking earth does he just want to parley."

"Curiously enough, on that point we're agreed." Talon might like the sound of his own voice, but negotiation didn't feature in his vocabulary. The guy was all about compliance, and he wasn't fussy about how he obtained said compliance. Either they were going to walk into a straight out attack, or the mad bastard had something particularly nasty up his sleeve. Whichever it was, Blaze was betting Asha was about to be flaunted as a bargaining chip, and that's what made it worth attending. It was their one chance to snatch her without wading into a pitch battle. The cathedral was too stacked with wards to plan an infiltration, and after his prior escape, he'd lay money on Talon having bolstered the defences.

"Blaze, there's more."

Ain't there always?

"The bit you reckoned Sorrow wouldn't mention. No demon's ever mated with a human before. They're fragile. There's no telling how it will affect her. The final act may kill her."

His guts knotted. There were lots of debates he could have with himself over the sensibility and morality of what he'd signed up for, but Asha was the one thing that was sacred in this. He couldn't lose her. And well, handing over her soul... That had to be her choice. Only he didn't trust the youkai not to muscle in on that decision.

"I've never known a human to survive

having a soul ripped away. I'm not saying I'm an expert on them, but, well... it's a concern."

Concern didn't come close to describing the torment raging inside him. He couldn't. He wouldn't sacrifice her. Frustrated, Blaze tore a hand through the waxed spikes of his hair.

"Do you know what the final step in this bonding ritual is?"

He'd avoid it, even if it meant he never got to hold Asha again. What other choice was there? He couldn't leave her with Talon. And yet, she was probably in more danger with him. One momentary lapse of concentration, another blood frenzy and he'd risk killing her himself.

"There must be documentation about the process. There are historical archives, aren't there?"

"Not exactly. There's not much cause for record keeping. We live a long time, there's not the same pressing urge to scribble everything down and pass on knowledge as there is with humans. We remember, and when we don't it's out of choice. Rebirth can be a defence mechanism, Blaze. Sometimes it's necessary to forget. Besides, even if there is documentation about the process, it doesn't apply here. She's human, that's the point. That's why it's risky. Youkai survive quite happily with one soul."

"Shit! This fucking sucks! I don't even know how I marked her." Only the fact that he could sense her shifting consciousness convinced him of the bond. Otherwise, he couldn't swear the mark hadn't been on her hand prior to their first meeting since most of the time she kept her gloves on.

"So it could be a touch, a kiss, sex?"

Raven gave a solemn nod.

"And this is my master plan, the reason I went through the whole rebirth thing. I must have been fucking nuts. Who the hell willingly signs up to fall in love and then sacrifice it? Please tell me I have a desk somewhere around here, and that I didn't just sit on my pompous arse out there in the audience chamber looking wan concocting this bullshit?"

"There's a desk, although you did do a fair amount of the latter. Actually, more fornicating than naval gazing."

His biography got better and better.

Raven came over and slapped Blaze's thigh. "Don't beat yourself up. You're our prince and you've always led by example. Besides, you're a damn good lay."

Blaze puckered up, snarled and blew him a kiss. "Desk—point me there."

"Through the secret door, just don't expect to find a document marked, 'Master Plan', 'cause there ain't going to be one."

"Great. In which case I think I'm going to go drum my head against a wall, and then get some kip before this showdown. How secret is this secret room? Is it quieter than my bedchamber?"

"Known only to you, me and yon crow over there." A small depiction of a crow backlit by a red sun lay hidden within the ashes from which the phoenix was rising. The same symbol his grandmother had had painted onto the shoulder of his leather jacket. Blaze took off the garment and laid it next to the one on the floor. They were identical down to the last detail. Raven passed him a signet ring, depicting the same thing again.

"You'll be needing this."

Blaze put on the ring, and passed his hand over the symbol, something clicked in the earth below, and a circular hole opened over a sheer drop. Unsteadily, he shuffled back from the edge.

"You've wings. You can fly. 'Course, it might be a little dusty down there. It has been fifty years."

"It's safe?"

"Blaze, nothing in this place is safe."

"Grubs?"

Raven stuck his head through the hole. "Not that I can smell, and they do have an almighty whiff to them, be it not quite on a par with Wisht Hounds."

8. DUSK

**
"Our tragedies are what form us."
– Gulielmus de Vere
**

FOUR OF THEM crossed the Division Bridge an hour before dusk—Blaze, flanked by Skaa, Sorrow, and Raven. Grace attempted to kiss Blaze goodbye, but he shuffled out of reach, and at least she didn't insist on forming part of his entourage. He had a feeling Grace hadn't entirely done with him yet.

"She'll never give in, you know," Raven said of the snake-like minx. "She's too used to getting her own way, and she doesn't understand how you could possibly be interested in a long term human lover."

Blaze couldn't keep the annoyance out of his voice. "Just because there's not a precedent. It's not like it's out and out weird, I've only been a demon a few days, and it's not as if I'm dating a harpy or a blooming wolf."

In many ways Raven's expression suggested as options went they might be preferable.

"Just because she was Talon," he continued. They stomped across the Division Bridge, Blaze almost oblivious to the fans of flame around him making up its railings and walkway.

"That's not it at all." Raven clapped an arm around his shoulder. "Her profession has nothing to do with this. It's more a case of simple biology. Trust me, I've dallied with the odd human in my time. Long term, they just don't work out."

"Right," Blaze huffed, shoulders still tensed up around his ears. Just what he needed, relationship advice from a demon—whom let's face it were predominately known for their rampant libidos and occasionally consuming human lovers whole.

"Lifespan is the major biggy. It's okay when they're twenty, forty even, but when they're eighty and you don't look any different to the day when you first met—then it gets weird."

So she'd age and he wouldn't. Yes, she was pretty, but it wasn't why he loved her. And maybe it would break his heart one day to have to let her go, but that wasn't a reason to walk away now.

"For another, they're fragile. They can't take the rough stuff in the same way we can, and it's easy to lose sight of that in the heat of passion."

Which presumably accounted for the tales of those bitten or devoured lovers? Blaze cocked an eyebrow to ask as much, only for Raven to mumble something incomprehensible in response, which might have been an affirmative, but could equally have been his latest take-out order.

"Okay." Blaze raised his hands and gave an exasperated sigh. "I get it, the odds are stacked against us. Doesn't mean I have to give up. I'm certainly not leaving her with Talon." Damn bastard alchemist had probably already had his filthy paws all over her.

Raven gave a curt nod, and scratched the side of his head. "I hear you. I'm just saying it how I see it. If it weren't for this bond mark, I'm telling you the relationship would be dead before it began."

Having reached the City side of the bridge, Raven unfolded the hideous weapon he had strapped across his back.

"Still got that gun in your pocket?"

"Yes. Reckon I should use it to put a hole in Talon?"

Raven waved him to a standstill, and checked the river bank despite Skaa and Sorrow already having passed ahead of them.

"Wish it were that easy. I figure it'll take something rather less discreet."

"Shotgun?" He should have picked up the one he had back home.

"I was thinking more along the lines of a canon. Something you can't dodge."

They crossed the shingle and headed into the marshland, keeping off the main road. No point in raising attention when they didn't have to. Even if the Talon weren't out hunting them, with the appearance of the castle in the sky over the Old City, tensions were probably running high among the City's inhabitants. And when people got spooked they tended to get a bit trigger happy. He didn't much fancy the idea of a bullet in the butt.

Blaze groaned as the sodden ground swallowed his boot up to the ankle. The whole area smelled like a herd of cattle had spent the afternoon having a farting contest. He clamped his sleeve over his nose, but the leather wasn't so great at keeping the smell out, nor did having his arm aloft help his gait through the bog.

"Couldn't we have just flown?"

Raven shook his head. "Skaa vetoed it."

"Yeah, and I've yet to work out why I'm listening to him." Blaze grumbled under his breath. Damn assassin. It wasn't, but it sure felt like this was all his fault.

They continued in silence for several minutes, until the marshland petered out and turned into waste ground littered with rubble. The silhouettes of the warehouses loomed on the horizon, squat wood and metal structures with weeds growing up through the cobblestones between the buildings. The roof of the nearest warehouse had collapsed in the right hand corner and the door hung on by the bottom hinge.

Skaa and Sorrow stood awaiting them in the shadow of a skeletal iron balcony. Blaze quickened his step to reach them—time they got this show over—only for Raven to tap him on the shoulder.

"Hold up a minute. I've something I want to ask you before we do this. I don't want to be getting my priorities wrong later."

"Go on." As Blaze nodded his assent, he noticed Skaa had turned to watch their approach. His black brows were drawn into a swooping V shape and an icy glint shone at the heart of his pupils.

"What's the plan regarding Asha? And I don't just mean the escape. Exactly how are you planning on dealing with—you know? If the fever hits you're going to be all over her."

"Simple," he piped up, although it sure as hell didn't seem simple. "You're going to make sure I keep my hands to myself."

Raven whistled through his teeth. "You don't like to ask for much, do you, my liege. And how exactly am I supposed to stop you?"

Blaze stepped in front of Raven, turning his back to Skaa. He didn't want a witness to this exchange. The fabric of Raven's shirt crumpled within his grip.

"You use whatever force or diversion necessary. I am not going to willingly sacrifice her to the youkai cause. I know you're all relying on me and jacking off over the idea of this triumvirate thing, but it's not happening if it's going to put her at risk."

He risked a quick glance at Skaa, who was still surveying them with the intensity of a hawk hunting a shrew.

"Until one of you can prove to me that she's going to be fine at the end of this, it's your job to make sure I don't so much as touch her. Got it?"

"All right, I hear you." Raven gave a curt nod. "I'll do what I can."

"Seriously, Raven, if you see me going near her with so much as a twinkle in my eye you'd better lay me out."

He couldn't actually read the thoughts running through Raven's head in that moment despite the blood bond formed through their exchange of fluids. Raven's thoughts were too tumultuous, and there were too many subtleties involved.

Much as Raven's mismatched eyes fascinated him, when the blowtorch lit in the heart of the right pupil, he knew it was time to turn away.

"Just don't get pissy with me, okay," he mumbled. "You can't expect me to take on all your world domination plans in one day. She's more important than that."

Raven curled his fingers over Blaze's shoulder. "They're your plans," he said softly. "You made them. We've been waiting countless human ages for this opportunity, so don't even think of bowing out. I understand your concern over Asha, but this is much bigger than one person."

Blaze shrugged off his hold and began walking towards the steps where the other two demons waited.

"We're talking about starting a war. The Talon aside, the population of this city aren't going to simply surrender without a fight. I'm not so sure I want that much blood on my hands. Don't know about you, but I can still see all the corpses on Hangover Street when I close my eyes, and then there are all the other potential atrocities to consider."

A dry chuckle welled from deep in his chief guard's throat. Then Raven's hand caught him hard across the back, jolting him forward.

"What are you talking about, Blaze? What sort of abuse are you going to sanction, exactly? Unless you're talking about what the bleeders have planned for us? We're under your command. Whatever you say goes. It doesn't have to be a wild free for all. Make up some rules."

"And they'll listen because?"

"Because you're their prince, and you're giving them what no one else can. Now chin up. I'd give my right wing to have the old Blaze back, but since I'm stuck with you... Well, let's see what we can make of this little charade." He grinned and strolled past Blaze. "All set? Have they arrived?" he called up to Sorrow and Skaa.

Sorrow pattered down the metal steps. "A couple of minutes ago. They went in around the back. She's with him, along with an escort of three."

"Makes us even," Raven mumbled.

"More or less."

As a tight group they left the shadows and approached the front of the building. Sorrow clasped the handle to the enormous shutter-like metal door. "Ready?"

He wasn't, but Blaze gave a nod anyway.

"Then let's go parley."

And hope the enormous hangar didn't go kaboom the moment they all stepped within.

9. GHOSTING

**

"Thus in a fit of despair,
and deprived of her Ci'th, she ghosted."
–Of Briar & Brimstone, Tales of the Old City.
**

THEY SHOULDN'T HAVE brought her along. Jaku watched Asha with a mixture of pity and revulsion. Heavens only knows why they had. Essentially mindless, if there remained a spark of the woman he'd fought with for the last five years, he couldn't see it, not in her expression, nor in the way she moved or acted. If they'd had to walk over to this foul meeting point—curiously only a hundred yards from where he'd found her the night before—then she would never have made it. His lithe agile partner had about as much balance as a gnat on roller-skates. If she moved, she stumbled. Talon had virtually carried her.

Any sane person could see that she needed to be tucked under a patchwork quilt in a rocking chair, but this was Talon, and sane wasn't necessarily the best descriptive.

Maybe it never had been. He'd certainly always been highly-strung and eccentric. However, before today Jaku had never bothered to open his eyes wide enough to notice exactly how off kilter some of what his boss spouted truly was. Of course, now he'd had his eyes opened, it was impossible to ignore exactly how deranged Talon's methods were.

From a deep pocket Jaku pulled a flask and gulped down a draft of Hunter's Cordial. The sharp explosion of chocolate and limes hit his tongue and he briefly closed his eyes, using the moment to centre himself and find a bit of inner peace. Hell knows what was really in the cordial but it always seemed to work. He opened his eyes again to find Ouran leaning towards him.

"I don't like this," the younger man muttered as he patted his hands together to ward off the cold. "Meeting with demons. It's not what we do. And why bring Asha along? No offence to your partner, but we could use another sword arm and she's cabbaged."

Kairn, the other hunter along for the ride placed a hand on each of their shoulders and shoved his head into their huddle, prompting Jaku to immediately back-step. He didn't know why Kairn had been chosen for this outing. He was still too raw and had no concept of personal boundaries. He also had stubble growing through the layers of pale foundation and powder caking his face.

"I heard they've poisoned her. That Makaresh gave her an experimental demon drug they're planning on feeding into the city water supply to help subjugate us all."

Ouran rolled his eyes, clearly incredulous.

"The only drug they need is themselves," Jaku remarked.

Kairn brushed off both responses as if they hadn't been made. Silly bleeder had shaved his eyebrows and drawn them on with pencil, which would have been fine, if he'd bothered to keep the stubble under control. The man needed some lessons in cosmetology. It would never do to have demon hunters running around looking like clowns after a night in the gutter. Their image played a big part in maintaining their status.

"So this isn't about negotiating an antidote out of them?"

Ouran immediately began coughing into his curled hand, barely masking his amusement at the remark.

"The hell it is. For starters there ain't no such thing as demon anti-venom and for seconds, Asha fucked up big time when she let Makaresh escape. Talon's more likely to feed her to them than start pleading for favours on her behalf." He paused to peer nervously around. Talon stood out of normal hearing range, an arm around Asha's slender waist. Not that distance could be relied upon to ensure Talon wasn't listening to every word passing between them.

"What's your take, Jaku? You brought her in. Guess you'll be looking for another partner."

What opinions he had weren't for sharing.

Not yet, anyway. Better he kept them rattling around in his head until they magically formed a whole he could actually stomach the thought of.

"Shit, they're here." Ouran tapped his upper arm, prompting Jaku to ready his halberd.

"They look—" Kairn paused to take a large breath, which he released as a whistle. "They look human."

"Of course they do, dumbo. They're hardly going to walk around in spiky chaos armour attracting attention when this is supposed to be secret, hush, hush, stuff, are they?"

"I just meant..."

"He's right, Ouran. This lot are different." Jaku sniffed. Only a trace of their scent drifted through the still air, but it was distinctly different to the normal whiff of youkai cologne, being richer, more exotic and altogether sexier. "I'm afraid these guys are the ones your mothers really ought to have warned you about instead of wasting their breaths over the scum we normally slaughter. You're not going to see any metamorphosis mishaps on these guys." No extra toes, or pupils that failed to dilate, nor smiles that ran over wide. None of the normal little hints they were all trained to look out for in order to detect the youkai hiding amongst the townsfolk. No, these guys were gorgeous in an abnormally perfect way. Flawless alabaster skin, dark, deep eyes, hair like a shroud of floating midnight. Okay, so the effect was magnified by seeing them all standing together, but...

"Fuck!" Still as eloquent as ever, Kairn's jaw dropped and stayed open.

Stupid third son of some high-ups in the Heights, he was only here because his mother had wanted a daughter. Too bad her son looked appalling in a dress.

"Quit gawping." Jaku nudged him in the ribs. "Try looking as if you could cause indigestion rather than make a pleasant breakfast."

Goldfish boy closed his mouth. Thankfully, the collective youkai gaze had fallen on Talon rather than them.

Talon stepped forward, blond hair curled around his shoulders, the ends of which were still stained blood-red. For once the sly alchemist wore more than a pair of trousers and a smile. He had on a white loose sleeved shirt and a brilliant green waistcoat.

"Blaze Makaresh. Sirs." Talon bowed, but kept his eyes focused upon the approaching youkai. "It's a pleasure to meet you again."

Blaze stopped about six feet away. No longer quite so fresh faced as he'd been, the last few days had chiselled strength into his jaw and given him a stone cold gaze.

"I won't lie and say the feeling's mutual. What is it you think we have to talk about, alchemist?"

His guard formed a wedge around him, one to the rear and one on either side. Hard to believe this was the boy he'd peeled off the pavement after the previous youkai captain had torn a piece out of his back.

"I have something you want."

The collective youkai eyebrows rose up their brows.

"You have nothing I want."

"Liar," Jaku spat, catching the tiny flick of Blaze's eyes in Asha's direction. He rushed forward catching hold of Asha's elbow on her exposed side. Talon still held her clasped against his body, as if that alone were keeping her upright. "Look what you've done to her. Isn't that enough?"

"What I've done to her? What exactly is it you think I've done, Jaku? Last time I saw her she was standing upright on her own just fine. It was her decision to leave me, not mine. Maybe you should direct your questions at Talon instead."

Bastard youkai scum.

If Blaze expected him to believe... the damned-demon smelled of her. He'd fed off her. Sacrificed her in order to fuel his growth. In a horrific imagining, he saw Blaze feeding from Asha, drawing on her blood and stealing bites of flesh along with her life essence.

Blaze thoughtfully pursed his lips.

"Blind loyalty, is that what it is that stops you from seeing the truth? Is that what dragged you back to him, Jaku? Can't you see he's a fraud and a liar? He's no more human that I am. Perhaps even less so, since I still possess a heart."

The scene in Jaku's head transformed into an image of Talon fucking Asha while he drip fed her his tainted blood. That was exactly what had occurred. Talon hadn't tried to cure her, only to bind her to his will instead of Blaze's.

"How much grovelling did he have you do?"

"I don't grovel," Jaku snarled in return, casting aside the truths of both visions. "And one misunderstanding doesn't counterbalance all the evils your race have inflicted upon us for time immemorial."

The demon on Blaze's right took a pace forward. "Your memories are unfortunately exceedingly short. How many of us have you killed and then snorted up your noses? You call us evil, but we rarely kill in order to satisfy our cravings. None of you can say the same."

"Raven." Blaze touched the demon's shoulder.

"I speak the truth. Why shouldn't they hear it? No more than a handful of humans have died due to us in the last century. The same cannot be said of them. They've killed far more of their own than we ever have. How many did you sacrifice yesterday?"

"Enough." The soft burr of Talon's voice cut through the noise, and rippled across the volatile emotions in the room, lending curious calm to all. "Let's return to business, shall we?"

He thrust Asha away from his body, pushing her forward over the cracked and pitted warehouse floor, so that she stood beneath the beam of one of the glowing blue orbs Talon had summoned for lighting.

"If your interest in her is so lax, why are you here, demon prince? Don't you think I'm astute enough to realise my offering her in exchange for your presence is the only reason you came?"

Blaze took a step forward, reaching out to Asha's frail form, but before he could touch her, the puddle of light in which she stood changed from blue to red and bars fizzled into being.

"What?" Jaku raised his hand to touch his master's arm, but the contact stung as if he'd been flayed. Indeed, when he looked down the skin had been stripped from his fingertips, and blood rolled along his digits to pool in his palm.

"Don't interrupt again."

"Asha—that was the agreement. Asha in exchange for my presence." Blaze's eyes flashed copper-red, before settling back to blue. "Didn't he tell you that bit, Jaku?"

Jaku slowly shook his head. Talon had deceived him again. He stared at his golden-haired master, anger brewing in his innards. Talon had always meant to hand Asha over, to use her like Ouran had suggested. She was nothing more than a pawn to him, a carrot to dangle and condemn. Blaze would take her home and feed on her one last time, leaving her already damaged shell completely broken.

"No!" Seething anger rolled up through his chest, released itself as a mighty push. He kept on trusting, allowing himself to be blinded and deceived. No more. He wouldn't let Talon do this. It made no sense anyway. The demons would never honour any bargain they struck. All they'd be doing was handing Blaze the supper he needed to completely annihilate them.

He barrelled into Talon's side, hoping to break his concentration long enough so that he could snatch Asha from within the cage and run. Instead, he stopped dead when he hit Talon's side. The impact numbed him. His bones locked, tendons stiffened, and then he dropped like a stone into a deep lake, black waves closing over his head as the lights went out.

PITY SCORED BLAZE's heart as he watched Jaku fall. He'd never entirely liked or understood Asha's demon-hunting partner, but he deserved a better master than Talon, who didn't even look down to note where his servant had fallen.

"I've honoured my part, now honour yours. Un-cage her, or we leave now," Blaze demanded.

"Without her?" Talon infused his voice with doubt. "I don't think so. No, we'll talk first and you can have her once we reach an accord."

Blaze ignored the knots of anxiety cramping up his stomach and focussed upon Talon's face. He dared not look at Asha. It was best he didn't get too close or touch her anyway. He had to leave her safety up to Raven and the others, trust they'd protect her when it was time to flee.

"You're mistaken. Unlike you I've no taste for bloodshed and war. I foolishly thought you actually intended this to be a discussion."

Talon's smile stretched across his narrow face, which completely lacked warmth or cordiality. "You want to discuss. Then let us discuss. What shall we begin with—a proposed cease in hostilities or do you want to compare notes on exactly how hot she is in bed?"

"If you've so much has harmed a—" He should have kept a cap on his temper, but the thought of Talon holding her, abusing her like that derailed his judgement.

"I'm not the one draining her." Talon shot back. "Matter of fact, I think my blood and the other essences I've fed her are all that's keeping her alive."

"You've fed her?" Horror threaded through Sorrow's voice, accompanied by a look of revolt. His lips peeled back off his sharpened teeth and his eyes squeezed down to narrow slits.

"Blaze, this is a mistake," Skaa, who stood to his rear, hissed over his shoulder.

"Hold your counsel." He held them back with a gesture. Opinions could wait, he had to maintain his focus on Talon, because, that was one thing he was sure of, Talon would exploit any crack in his defence, any and every one. "What do you want?"

"The Old City is mine. Too long we've been ruled from the Heights. It's time we stood strong together and changed that, but not for demon rule. Take your little posse home and remove your castle from the sky. Let the Blood Moon usher in the only regime change this city needs."

"And for that you offer me a tormented woman who can barely support her own weight." Blaze forced a laugh, even though his guts and diaphragm protested the effort. "It's hardly a tempting deal."

He'd broken one of Talon's ensorcelled cages before. There was no reason to suppose he couldn't do it again in order to free Asha. He simply needed to find a way to distract Talon long enough for him to focus on the task without raising suspicions. Shame he couldn't think of one way of doing that. Instead his focus kept slipping towards the cage. He'd moved without realising it, so that if he reached through the bars he could touch her wan cheek and entwine his fingers in her hair. Her scent reached his nostrils. Desire flared—hot, hungry and immediate.

Want...

His guards moved in around him, hands twitching upon the hilts of weapons.

"Try again. What else have you to offer?"

He caught sight of her eyes in that moment, and made the mistake of holding her gaze. Hell's bollocks, but she was fading fast. He felt the silent plea of her soul. Asha lifted her palm towards him, held it outstretched.

"Make me another offer, or this meeting is over."

"It's already over." The bars of the cage fizzled away in a stream of hissing sparks.

Propelled by fate, Blaze took another step towards her, aware of Raven shadowing him so closely he could sense the tension in the big guy's limbs.

"Blaze," Raven's plea whistled past his ear.

It made him think long enough to pause. Long enough for Talon to snap out of focus and reappear at Asha's side.

"Well, if she's of no value to you—"

So fast. Too fast. He'd barely had time to register the weapon let alone consider where the sick bastard had got it from.

"—there's no point in keeping her around."

"No!" The echo of his cry reverberated in his ears, joined by another voice and then another. "No!" But the collective cry did nothing. Time seemed to freeze, then snap forward. Talon's sword came down clean and fast. Her head rolled just as Blaze caught her lifeless body. Blood gushed up over his face and splattered his clothes. "No." This couldn't be. It simply couldn't.

He held Asha, watched Talon laughing, and shock bleed across the faces of his remaining Dolls.

Why invite him here to do this? Why kill her? It made no sense.

Why kill her?

Blaze's head drooped. The weight of her body remained in his arms, but her lifeless eyes stared up at him from where her head had fallen. The one image sent his central nervous system into meltdown. The heat drained from his body as Asha's drained of blood. Numbness set in, slowing his heart until it almost stopped.

Cells started screaming for oxygen, and a popping sensation began in his brain.

It couldn't be. It seriously couldn't be.

He'd kill Talon. End this here and now.

The world would fare better without either of them meddling in affairs.

Blaze sank to the floor still cradling her body, his consciousness slipping back into the void and thence to the dead zone on the cathedral roof.

"Fuck!" Raven bellowed. It was the only word that came close to describing the current situation. Fuck! Fuck! And fucking bollocks! Talk about failure of epic proportions. Raven hadn't even seen that one coming. He bloody ought to have.

"Raven." Skaa's caw broke through the chief guard's litany of cursing. *What now?* Because he really didn't need any further woes. "Your man's down. Get him out of here."

Raven snapped to attention. Blaze had damn well zoned out again. His prince was sure making a habit of it. He was going to be dire at leading anyone into battle if he kept falling back on this act. Talon already stood over him, sword raised for the kill, a maniacal grin contorting his face.

Raven dived forward. He thumped Blaze hard between the shoulder blades, rolled around him, and swung at Talon, but the alchemist had already blinked out of reach. The knock had done the trick on Blaze though. The hiss of indrawn breath told him his prince's lungs were functioning, as did the wail of utter despair.

Like a match set to gasoline, flames leapt up in a ring around Blaze. Further jets burst from the ground like marsh lights. Purple flames licked up the walls, turned amber and green as they fanned out, until the roof glowed like a giant solar grill.

"Blaze, stop it." Raven left off chasing Talon, and returned to Blaze, shaking him hard. "Stop it. Focus. "

Unless he woke up, he was going to incinerate them all.

"Kill Talon. That's who you want."

Asha's body slipped from Blaze's grip as he turned to shove Raven away. Although the contact was brief, his hands burned clean through Raven's leather breastplate, and melted the skin beneath.

Pain flared, white hot and stinging, raw as any knife wound he'd ever had and more intense than when Asha had ripped the razor vines from his chest. Raven screamed. Knowing it would heal never helped with the shock of how bad it hurt.

Behind him Skaa's cackle filled the now smoke-enshrouded room. Raven turned to see Sorrow, worry lines scored across his forehead, stumble forward, beseeching his brother.

"It's started. She came through," Skaa virtually sang, his voice so filled with jubilant emotion they'd all be forgiven for thinking he'd lost it along with Blaze. "I never thought it would happen. But he's claimed her." Skaa turned his attention to Talon, whose watchful gaze focussed upon the flames continuing to flare around Blaze. Bastard was waiting for an opportunity. That's the only reason he hadn't already flown. "You fool," Skaa continued. "You've done what he never could, and what we were forbidden to do. You've given us our Prince."

"Then tell me why he despairs, demon." Talon remained rigidly composed. His two hunters, eyed the flames with increasing nervousness. "I've severed the link between them. He can no longer draw upon her strength or use her as a conduit. He can't suck up her power anymore." A smile briefly flickered across Talon's face and twinkled in the depths of his tear-shaped pupils.

Skaa laughed even harder. "All you've severed is her connection to the Earth. You've cemented the bond between them for eternity. You've given him her soul, alchemist. The one thing he would never have taken for himself."

"What?" A flash of concern briefly culled Talon's triumph.

"He knew it would kill her." Skaa paused dramatically, a smile now stretching his narrow face from cheek to cheek. "He was prepared to sacrifice a millennium of youkai rule to spend a few decades with her. We all knew it, and couldn't do a thing about it." He turned his irritating smile upon Raven, whose lips curled into a snarl. The charred scent of his own burnt flesh still filled his nostrils and the entire surface of his chest stung like someone had taken a cheese grater to it. "Wasn't that the discussion you had? Save the alchemist's whore, and screw the triumvirate?"

"It changes nothing." Talon began to back-step.

But truly it had changed everything.

"The city remains mine. A few sparks and a tantrum don't change that."

Sparks that were now a sheets of solid flame. Noxious gases swirled around their heads. The exposed skin of Raven's face stretched tight, as if he'd stood too long in the summer sun. They were all going to burn. Blaze would fill the sky with ashes.

Skaa and Sorrow lunged around him towards Talon, only to collide with a sheet of purple sparks. It flared briefly, repelling them both before the magic shattered. They lurched forward again, but too late. Talon soared upwards—white wings beating fast—through the clouds of smoke, and the tendrils of flame eating at the roof, leaving them all staring up at him in shock.

"Youkai!" Tears chased down the cheeks of the two demon-hunters Talon left behind, leaving tracks in their powdery make-up. "He's one of us."

Shock hit them, each and every one. Everyone except Blaze, who with a twist of his wrist calmly ripped away a section of crumbling roof and from a distance of thirty feet set light to Talon's flight feathers. Then, grim smile fixed in place he turned his gaze to Talon's bewildered entourage and calmly ignited their clothes. They ran, fleeing into the chill air outside the warehouse, howling in outrage, while trying to strip off clothing, and drop and roll.

In the sky, Talon pitched sideways losing height, his screams those of frustration rather than pain. The bastard would probably live. But they wouldn't, not unless they got out now. Another section of roofing collapsed, raining pieces of tiles and wood cinders down upon their heads.

"Blaze, please. Stop. We have to leave." He reached out to his friend, only to have his sleeve set alight. Wincing, Raven held onto Blaze. "At least let us honour her sacrifice. If we all die here, then Talon has won."

Sorrow muscled in behind him. "Her body," he ordered.

"Got it." Skaa scooped Asha's fallen form off the floor and ran for the door. "Burning Prince," he muttered. "He's erupting like a fucking volcano."

"Just get her out." Raven dragged Blaze towards the door. Sorrow took their prince's other arm, and together they managed to stumble into the fresh air.

"What about him?" Sorrow asked, looking back to where Jaku remained unconscious on the floor.

"Bring him. We might get some information

out of him. This is only the beginning. The war's still to be won."

AUTHOR'S NOTE

F YOU'RE SCREAMING in frustration along with Blaze, I'm sorry. I promise that Asha and Blaze's story isn't over yet. To quote Raven, "This is only the beginning." Discover what comes next in Blood Moon:Shadow Queen

ABOUT THE AUTHOR

MADELYNNE IS A New York Times & USA Today bestselling author. She wrote her first novel after discovering Black Lace Books in the 1990s. After escaping the Hotel California, she dived into storytelling full time. Her books are filled with bisexual bad boys who like to get down and dirty, and stories so angst-filled you know they're going to hurt.

She lives in the UK near the Welsh border, where you can find her surrounded by books, drinking rapidly cooling decaf coffee, and listening to loud music.

Come hang out with her via her newsletter, where she shares what she's reading, watching, listening to, and snippets about her current projects.